## *"About our marriage..."*

Jessica murmured. "What, besides the money, are you expecting from it?"

"No entanglements," Brody said in a low, ominous tone, his face darkening.

That meant no intimacy, Jessica assumed. To her chaste chagrin, she didn't know whether she was hurt or relieved. She'd heard that winters were long and cold in Colorado, where she and her *husband* would be holed up.

Brody continued to gaze at her, his eyes dark pools filled with secrets too dire for her to know. A shiver plunged down her spine, and for a moment she knew real fear.

This lean, muscled bodyguard of hers was danger personified. Yet she was trusting him with her very life.

What she didn't know...was why.

Dear Reader,

The hustle and bustle of the holiday season is just around the corner—and Special Edition's November lineup promises to provide the perfect diversion!

This month's THAT SPECIAL WOMAN! title is brought to you by veteran author Lindsay McKenna. *White Wolf* takes you on a stirring, spiritual journey with a mystical Native American medicine woman who falls helplessly in love with the hardened hero she's destined to heal!

Not to be missed is *The Ranger and the Schoolmarm* by Penny Richards—the first book in the SWITCHED AT BIRTH miniseries. A collaborative effort with Suzannah Davis, this compelling series is about four men...switched at birth!

And bestselling author Anne McAllister delivers book six in the CODE OF THE WEST series with *A Cowboy's Tears*—a heartfelt, deeply emotional tale. The first five books in the series were Silhouette Desire titles.

The romance continues with *The Paternity Test* by Pamela Toth when a well-meaning nanny succumbs to the irresistible charms of her boss—and discovers she's pregnant! And Laurie Paige serves up a rollicking marriage-of-convenience story that will leave you on the edge of your seat in *Husband: Bought and Paid For.*

Finally, *Mountain Man* by Silhouette newcomer Doris Rangel transports you to a rugged mountaintop where man, woman and child learn the meaning of trust—and discover unexpected happiness!

I hope you enjoy all that we have in store for you this November. Happy Thanksgiving Day—and all of us at Silhouette would like to wish you a joyous holiday season!

Sincerely,

Tara Gavin
Senior Editor

---

Please address questions and book requests to:
Silhouette Reader Service
U.S.: 3010 Walden Ave., P.O. Box 1325, Buffalo, NY 14269
Canadian: P.O. Box 609, Fort Erie, Ont. L2A 5X3

# LAURIE PAIGE

## HUSBAND: BOUGHT AND PAID FOR

Published by Silhouette Books
America's Publisher of Contemporary Romance

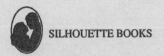

SILHOUETTE BOOKS

ISBN 0-373-24139-9

HUSBAND: BOUGHT AND PAID FOR

**Printed in U.S.A.**

**Books by Laurie Paige**

Silhouette Special Edition

*Lover's Choice* #170
*Man Without a Past* #755
† *Home for a Wild Heart* #828
†*A Place for Eagles* #839
†*The Way of a Man* #849
†*Wild Is the Wind* #887
†*A River To Cross* #910
*Molly Darling* #1021
*Live-In Mom* #1077
*The Ready-Made Family* #1114
*Husband: Bought and*
  *Paid For* #1139

Silhouette Desire

*Gypsy Enchantment* #123
*Journey to Desire* #195
*Misty Splendor* #304
*Golden Promise* #404

Silhouette Yours Truly

*Christmas Kisses for a Dollar*
*Only One Groom Allowed*

Silhouette Romance

*South of the Sun* #296
*A Tangle of Rainbows* #333
*A Season for Butterflies* #364
*Nothing Lost* #382
*The Sea at Dawn* #398
*A Season for Homecoming* #727
*Home Fires Burning Bright* #733
*Man from the North Country* #772
\*Cara's Beloved* #917
\*Sally's Beau* #923
\*Victoria's Conquest* #933
*Caleb's Son* #994
†*A Rogue's Heart* #1013
*An Unexpected Delivery* #1151
*Wanted: One Son* #1246

Silhouette Books

Montana Mavericks
*The Once and Future Wife*
*Father Found*

*All-American Sweethearts
†Wild River

## LAURIE PAIGE

was recently presented with the *Affaire de Coeur* Readers' Choice Silver Pen Award for Favorite Contemporary Author. In addition, she was a 1994 Romance Writers of America RITA Award finalist for Best Traditional Romance for her book *Sally's Beau.* She reports romance is blooming in her part of northern California. With the birth of her second grandson, she finds herself madly in love with three wonderful males—"all hero material." So far, her husband hasn't complained about the other men in her life.

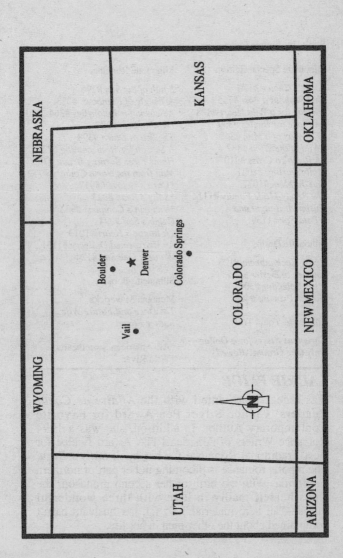

# Chapter One

Jessica Lockhart rested her forehead against the wall-to-wall-plate-glass window and stared at the Chicago traffic on the street forty-five stories below. She sighed. Her breath appeared briefly on the cool pane as a circle of moisture. The glass echoed the sigh back to her so that she heard the sound at the same instant.

The city was busy on this chilling March night.

Headlights swept a path through the dark for the vehicles that rushed along the streets as if they were strange insects, each scurrying to do their important deeds before dawn broke. She glanced at her watch. Almost two.

She stood on an observation platform that was part of a skywalk overlooking an atrium two floors below. Through the hazy glow of light reflecting from the window, she could see the fig trees swaying with the stir of warm air from the registers. The image of her body-guard was also reflected in the window.

Brody Smith. Private Investigator. Partner in a small security agency that handled special cases and only by referral. Thanks to a large inheritance, her trustees could afford the best for her.

The thought sounded cynical, even to her. Money was supposed to make life easier. And it did. She wasn't stupid when it came to economics. But it was also a burden.

She watched as Brody glanced around the area. His dark gaze lingered on her. He was probably wondering how much longer she was going to stand there staring out at the night.

The atrium skywalk was her favorite spot to contemplate life. It suited her, this high and lonely place.

In the glass, his image stood, then stretched. He rotated his shoulders as if they were stiff. He was a tall, lean man with black hair and eyes so dark they, too, seemed black. He rarely smiled, but when he did, it changed his rough features in a manner that was startling.

Not that he became handsome. He'd lived a hard life. It showed in a nose that had been broken—twice, he'd said with that cynical, so-what? smile he used when she pried into his personal life. Along his right temple, the flesh was puckered into a narrow scar an inch long. A bullet that someone had tried to put his name on, he'd told her.

The scar gave him a somewhat forbidding look. It told the observer that here was a man who wasn't afraid of life.

By contrast, his smiles, when they came, were sudden and breath-catching. He had beautiful teeth, perfectly straight and very white against his swarthy skin. He'd come by them naturally. She'd had to pay a fortune for her straight smile.

She sighed again, knowing it was time to go home for the night. Home was her grandfather's estate an hour's drive from downtown, where she'd lived for the past six months. She turned slowly, regretting the intrusion of reality. "Shall we go?"

"When you're ready."

No emotion stirred the rich timbre of his voice, neither impatience nor irritation. She wondered what would stir him.

Perhaps if she made a pass? No, he'd give her that dead-level stare as if he hadn't a clue to what she meant. Neither anger nor passion would light his eyes.

That was no particular obstacle to her plans.

She faced the window again. Putting her palms against the pane, she felt the cold seep into her hands. An urge to strike the glass came over her. She hit it with the heel of her fist, but not terribly hard. The blow was intended to state her defiance, not to inflict damage. The strength of the tempered glass was greater than any brute force she could muster.

There were times of late that she'd thought of herself as a bird in a glass cage, beating her wings uselessly against a fate she couldn't change.

"If I marry," she said, "that would solve all my problems, wouldn't it?"

In the night-framed window, she saw his gaze swing to her as if it were a heat-seeking missile locking on target.

"That depends on the guy you marry."

She ignored the sardonic twist to the words. "I

meant as far as the inheritance goes. I'd be free of my mother's will."

The private investigator strode the perimeter of the observation platform, his gaze alert for the slightest sign of danger. The trustees thought someone was trying to kill her. Actually they thought her uncle was the culprit. He would inherit her trust fund if she died without heirs.

"Only if you stay married for one year."

"Yes. A year. That's not so much out of a person's life. Not when you look at how long people live nowadays."

He gave a noncommittal, "Huh."

She faced him again. "After one year, I'd be free to leave the money to anyone I wanted. Or to a charity."

"At thirty-five, you'll inherit without having to marry," he reminded her. He watched her with the wary expression of a man who had braved danger often in his life and knew its signs well.

"That's years from now. I want to be free."

He nodded his head, an almost imperceptible movement, and his eyes narrowed. He wasn't going to help her out.

"I've been living with a bodyguard for almost a year. To face nine more years of it..." She shook her head in refusal.

"Someone tried to kill you," he reminded her.

"The police think they were accidents." She was grasping at straws.

"How many of these accidents have you had?" he questioned, goading her into remembering the strange occurrences in her life since she'd turned twenty-five and could presumably take control of her inheritance by staying married for one year. If she died before that event took place or before she turned thirty-five, her uncle stood to gain everything.

"Shortly after my birthday, my brakes failed. The fluid had leaked out. Fortunately I always step on the brake pedal when I start the car. It went down to the floor, so I knew I had no brakes. The mechanic found the line might have been cut."

She fell silent, remembering that the police had been called in to investigate. They'd found an ID medallion belonging to her uncle's gardener, who had mysteriously disappeared, near where she'd been parked. But there hadn't been anything that could prove her uncle's guilt—or innocence. Uncle Jesse had accused her grandfather of trying to frame him. There was no love lost between the two men.

Nor had there been between her mother and her grandfather—stepgrandfather, actually. Her mother had left the older man out of her will. She and Uncle Jesse had never accepted him in their real father's place.

However, he was the only grandfather Jessica had ever known. He'd taken her in as a twelve-year-old orphan and raised her. For that she would always be grateful. He was also one of her trustees since Mr. Parker of the original three had died.

"And after that?" Brody prodded.

"Someone forced me off the road one snowy night. I thought the driver was the gardener. Since then I've tried two security agencies, neither very satisfactory." A chill crept around her heart as she told of the mishaps.

"You rebelled last month and fired the last guy."

"It was a she. I caught her going through the clothes in my bureau. She was nosy and intrusive."

"During your bid for freedom, the steering came

loose in your car, which is less than a year old. You were lucky to be able to stop before you hit a concrete embankment. Your uncle's fingerprints were on the car. You said you'd talked to him at a charity ball and he'd leaned against your car.''

"He did.''

She gripped the railing. It was daunting to realize her relative might be plotting to kill her. "A friend's husband recommended you. He said you would ferret out the truth if it was possible to do so. You've been here three weeks without results. The other agencies didn't find anything in eight months. I've thought of another solution, an easier one." Her smile was brittle. "I simply need to marry.''

"For one year.''

She met his dark, moody gaze and directed a challenge to him. "Don't you think I can make it through a year?''

"No.''

The blunt reply sent a wave of heat through her. Anger warred with humiliation. "I didn't realize your opinion of me was quite so low.''

He shrugged. "Don't ask if you don't want an answer.''

"I'll remember that in the future." She clutched her tiny evening bag against her chest and headed for the elevator door.

Brody fell into step beside her. She walked faster. He kept up effortlessly.

At the elevator, he punched in the code. The door slid open. He checked it before letting her enter.

She stepped in and pulled the silver fox—a remade jacket from one of her grandmother's coats—close around her, burying her nose in it so he wouldn't see the color in her cheeks.

In the parking garage, he checked the car out as carefully as the elevator although the longtime family driver was inside and had been there since they'd arrived an hour ago.

Guilt for keeping them out so late added to her inner turmoil. However, she'd needed the quiet. As chairperson of a charity ball, she'd spent most of the evening in a crowd, Brody's disapproving presence always at her side. A friend had flirted shamelessly with him every chance she got. Brody had paid absolutely no attention.

That's when Jessica had gotten her brilliant idea. Brody was in his early thirties. The fact that he wasn't married and seemed quite free to follow her around and investigate her life and friends suggested to her that he might be willing to go along with the idea of marriage.

When they were well on their way to the country house, she drew a deep breath and plunged in. "Would you be willing to marry me for a year?"

He gazed at her for what seemed to be ages. "No."

She'd thought she was prepared for a denial, but still she was surprised when tears stung her eyes. "I'd pay you well. Your regular salary plus a bonus equal to the same amount."

"No."

She forced herself to look upon the proposal as a business deal, which it was, not as a personal matter between them, which it wasn't. "All right," she said, injecting a smidgen of resigned humor in the words. "I'll double your salary. And the bonus. Isn't that enough for one year of your time?"

"It isn't the money."

"Then what is it?"

"I don't want the entanglements that marriage brings."

"It isn't as if it would be a real marriage. You'd make a lot of money and I...maybe I would have a life."

"You don't now?"

She glared at him. "No. Not with you around."

"This to the guy she just asked to marry her," he murmured, one dark eyebrow lifting as he mocked her suggestion.

"Since I turned twenty-five and someone decided to play tricks with my life, I've not had one. Until I marry, the trustees insist that I keep you on. Or, if not you, another just like you," she added glumly. She gazed out the windows as snow began to fall. More and more, the luxury in which she lived seemed like a cage, gilded, yes, but a cage nevertheless.

"Nice that you can distinguish between us."

This time she heard the slice of humor served with the cynicism. "Sorry, I didn't mean to be insulting."

Ironically Brody was the one person she did trust. She did it instinctively. He seemed to know exactly what he was doing and why. At times, she'd found his presence comforting.

But the fact was she hadn't had a moment alone in ages. Never alone, but always lonely. Oh, stop feeling sorry for yourself, she mentally chided.

"I'm serious about marriage, Brody. That would solve the problem since the trustees won't let me give any money to Uncle Jesse. One year of marriage and they're out of the picture."

"Will you give your inheritance to your uncle?" Brody asked on a curious note.

"I don't know," she said honestly. "I loved him when I was a child. When he came to visit, we had a great time. My mother thought he was wonderful, but he wasn't very good at holding a job. She used to give him money. It made my grandfather angry. I remember they quarreled about it once when he invited us home for Christmas. He said my uncle was no good. That made my mother furious and we left."

"But you were sent to live with your grandfather when your mother died?" Brody knew the facts of her life, but he sometimes asked questions as if not clear on a particular point.

Jessica nodded. "My mother set up the trust fund with the law firm and the bank, but she didn't say where I was to live. I guess she didn't expect to get cancer and die in eight months. There was a custody hearing, then I came here to live. My uncle had charm but not much else. He'd made a lot of bad investments."

"Did he say that?" Brody asked.

"No. Grandfather told me."

"Your uncle seems to live well."

Her hackles rose. She was defensive about her uncle. He had a different life-style, but she found it hard to believe he would try to harm her. "He's found his niche."

"And a partner who's quite wealthy."

A chill went down her spine. Brody's voice was deep, with ominous undertones that conveyed an intimate knowledge of the sinister side of life. She peered at him, trying to guess his meaning from his expression. Naturally she couldn't.

"Are you insinuating Uncle Jesse's partner has something to worry about?"

"I never insinuate."

The flat statement stilled further arguments from her. Brody didn't trust anyone. That much was clear. She touched the car window and felt the coldness creeping near, one thin slice of glass away. A shiver ran over her.

"Are you cold?" he asked, his hand already on the controls.

She shook her head and dropped her hand to her lap. "Sometimes the cold seems to be waiting," she said. "Like the Snow Queen, if it touches a person, it turns one's heart to ice."

"Poor little rich girl."

She clenched her cold hands on her purse and managed a laugh. "Not at all. I only have to find a husband. Then all my troubles will be over. And you'll be out of a cushy job."

Brody walked the perimeter of the terrace that surrounded the country estate. All the security devices were on and working properly. He moved his shoulders, irritated at the tightness across his back and up his neck.

Tension.

A certain amount was good. A man had to stay alert. But this wasn't that kind of strain.

A cynical smile flitted over his mouth. He knew what the problem was, had known the moment he walked into the office where the attorney, a longtime friend, had introduced Brody to Jessica Lacey Lockhart, and his sense of caution and preservation had gone at once on red-alert.

He knew danger when it came at him with a curvy body, wind-tossed, sun-streaked hair and a smile that belied the trace of vulnerability in gray eyes as translucent as rain. He'd taken the case, against his better judgment, but he'd taken it.

Now—marriage.

He should have cut and run when he'd still had the chance, that first moment in the law office. Now he couldn't. It was a failing of his—this concern for the underdog, for anyone not quite dealt a fair hand.

Jessica fell into that category. She paid a price for her privileged life.

He stretched and rubbed the back of his neck with one hand. A yearning to be in Colorado, riding his land, breathing the cold mountain air, swept over him. A man felt free there, not constrained by the constant press of humanity found in the city.

Walking around the corner of the century-old brick mansion, he checked the digital readout on the security monitor, clicked off the LED display and replaced the device in his jacket pocket. He paused and looked at the light falling from a bedroom window.

Jessica's room.

For a moment, he wondered if she'd experience the sense of freedom he did on the ranch he'd bought with his life savings and visited whenever he could. With his office in Denver and his work taking him all over the States, he didn't get there as often as he'd like.

That would change soon. The ranch was breaking even, sometimes making a small profit, and he nearly had enough money to retire from active cases. He could run the agency from the ranch for him and his partner. They could take in an associate in his place. The money Jessica had mentioned would be enough to do it.

He gave a start of surprise. He was considering her offer. He was really considering her offer.

Was he out of his ever-loving mind?

A movement in her room drew his attention. He quickly checked the open slope of lawn that ran to the perimeter fence. No signs of an interloper. At the ranch, other than a coyote or an occasional mountain lion, he could go days without seeing another living soul. He liked it that way.

When he turned back to the French doors, he saw Jessica standing there, her expression pensive as she gazed out at the night. She wore a white, silky-looking nightgown with a lacy robe over it. Her short curly hair, backlighted by the bedside lamp, formed a halo around her head.

She looked like an angel, but he knew that someday she would be some man's downfall. He wasn't going to be that man.

When he moved from the shadows into the light, she drew back, a hand to her breast, then relaxed when she saw who it was.

They watched each other through the glass for a long ten seconds, then she flicked the dead bolt and opened the door.

"All quiet in the OK Corral, Sheriff?" she asked, one slender eyebrow arched slightly.

"Yeah." He checked the room, then let his gaze drift slowly over her. She was a curvy woman with a small waist, but flaring hips and full breasts. The innocence in her eyes didn't go with that body that was nothing but temptation in the flesh.

He glanced down. That's when he noticed her feet were bare. Her toes were the daintiest things he'd ever seen, rounded and pink with pale polish on the manicured nails.

He got an ache in certain places that wouldn't quit.

He gave an irritated snort at his eager response to a woman who saw him only as a way out of her predicament. He quickly checked to make sure he didn't shock her with his body's flagrant behavior.

When he looked up, it was in time to catch her gaze following his. Her eyelashes flickered before she raised her gaze upward again.

"I was wondering earlier what it would take to stir you," she said in a husky murmur.

She had an eyebrow with an attitude. It lifted slightly in mocking humor at his discomfort. His response to her was obvious behind the fly of the jeans he'd changed to before making his nightly rounds of the security system.

He gestured with one hand. "Night. A bedroom. A woman ready for bed. That's about what it takes for any man." He managed to keep his voice from dropping to a register of hoarse desire, although his blood pulsed with it.

Her scent pervaded the room. She smelled sexy—of perfume and powder and a woman's secret spice. His nostrils flared as he dragged air into his lungs.

For two cents, he'd sweep her into his arms and they'd both land in that prissy white bed with its jumble of pillows covered in delicate eyelet lace pillowcases and matching sheets.

Yeah, that would be a real smart thing to do.

"Change your mind about the money?" she asked.

It took him an instant to figure out what she was talking about. "The marriage proposition," he confirmed.

"Yes."

"No way am I going to be suckered into that

noose.'' He stuck his fingers into his back pockets with the intention of keeping them there.

A tide of pink crept up her neck and settled in her cheeks, but her smile was as cool as an icicle. ''Too bad.''

''What's wrong with one of those society guys at the ball tonight?''

''I don't trust them.''

Her eyes issued a challenge that for a moment he wanted to accept. He controlled himself with an effort. ''The implication being that I'm honorable and all that. Sorry, but that form of manipulation won't work, either.''

He couldn't help but think of a form that would. All she had to do was step close and press those high, bouncy breasts against him and he'd probably roll over and let her walk on him if she wanted to.

Jessica shook her head in exasperation. Brody weighed every word she said, then used it against her. Odd, to be so trustworthy himself, yet not to trust anyone else. Psychology class had taught her that most people suspected others of their own sins. Not Brody. He trusted no one on general principle.

''If an appeal to your better instincts won't work, what will?'' she asked boldly. She liked the idea of solving her problem with Brody. As her husband, he could continue his job of protecting her at a darned good wage, then after a year...

A year of being married to Brody. It occurred to her to wonder just what else he would expect as her husband. And what she would be willing to give.

Sex?

Would she be willing to exchange her body for the security of marriage to him? Women had done so since

Day One for the same or less. She instinctively knew she would get much more than security from him. Brody would know how to please a woman. He was too virile, too much a man not to be considerate of his partner. He'd see that his woman was satisfied before seeking his own total pleasure.

A delicate heat infused her skin as if someone had turned a furnace on inside her. She held his gaze with an effort and stood her ground as he moved closer.

He reached out and ran a finger along the lacy edge of her peignoir. "What do you call this?" he asked on a deep note.

An electrical shock ran through her, dropping deep into an abyss of need she'd rarely allowed to surface. She found herself wondering about his kiss and how it would feel, and exactly how he would touch a woman in passion.

She knew he was aroused. It wasn't something he could hide in those jeans that fit like skin and with a short jacket over them. Gazing into his dark eyes, she saw other passions as fleeting as a mist in sunshine. He was a man of caution.

"A peignoir," she said flippantly, pushing his hand aside.

"A temptation," he said, correcting her. "One I don't intend to try." He spun and headed for the door.

"Coward," she said softly.

He stopped but stayed with his back to her. "Or maybe I'm just not that desperate yet." He walked out.

When he stood on the other side of the door, she watched him, puzzled. He rattled the door. Oh. She went over and snapped the dead bolt into place. He tried the knob, nodded and disappeared into the darkness.

Jessica sank into her favorite chair. Weakness rushed over her as if she'd faced down a terrible danger. Her head ached above her eyes and at the back of her neck. She rubbed her temples absently.

She went through all the men friends she had. There weren't many. Her grandfather had sent her to an all-girls prep school in Virginia. She still wrote to a couple of girlfriends from those days. At her grandfather's urging, she'd attended her grandmother's alma mater, an all-female college back east.

When she'd mentioned joining the Peace Corps after college, her trustees had been horrified. Surprisingly her grandfather had taken her side when she'd wanted to go to other countries and teach health classes as part of a foundation grant sponsored by a missionary couple. The four young women who had volunteered had been strictly chaperoned. After three years, she'd come down with a new strain of malaria and returned home.

She realized she'd hardly been in Chicago long enough to meet any adults her age, much less form lasting friendships, until this past year.

Her acquaintances now were mostly the bankers and attorneys who handled her trust and directed the atrium building and other properties, which were part of her holdings. She knew lots of people from her charity work, but none as close friends.

She'd had one near-serious relationship: a young doctor on an intern program. He'd quarreled with a resident physician and been dismissed in disgrace. He'd left the area.

Having a bodyguard cast a pall on any relationship. Brody, with his dark scowls and sharp scrutiny, would make the devil himself run for cover. If he wouldn't marry her, not even for money, who would?

* * *

Brody paced his unlit room, feeling as if he were a caged panther who needed to prowl. He still felt a sense of shock that Jessica Lockhart, heiress, had suggested marriage.

To him. Brody Smith, the kid that nobody had wanted. His own mother had deserted him when he'd been fourteen.

*I love you, hon, but I got to go. Bill wants me to come with him, but there's no room for you. You're big for your age. You'll do fine.*

She'd given him a twenty-dollar bill and put him on a bus to a small town where a distant relative was to take him in. He'd arrived there two years later, older and a lot wiser for his time on the road. His foster sister, an orphan whose parents had been killed in an auto accident, had already been in residence at his great-aunt's house. He'd never seen his mother again. She'd died in a fiery crash a few months after sending him on his way.

Aunt Essie was dead now, too. Carly was married to a rancher in California. Things hadn't been easy for her. She'd trusted one man who had turned out to be a liar. But the second one had been okay, in spite of an earlier divorce. He'd checked out the guy himself.

Unable to stand the confines of the room, he went outside and surveyed the perimeter of the house once more. The landscape was coldly beautiful under the glow of the winter moon that had risen and now hung low on the horizon.

On the eastern side of the house, Jessica's bedroom was dark. She'd gone to bed.

At once a picture of her in the bed came to him. White on white, her gown against the sheets. Her tousled curls, artfully streaked at the best shop—he knew because he went there with her, although they'd tried to make him wait outside—would be spread in disarray over the pillow...

He grimaced as pleasure-pain danced through him, filling him with needs that drove him on his restless, nocturnal meandering. He frowned at the dark doors, then realized someone was staring back at him.

Jessica. Standing there in her white gown, looking like a fairy princess come to life. Her outrageous request hummed through his mind. He obviously was a man who looked as if he could be bought.

Maybe he could.

He went to the door. The dead bolt snicked open. He went inside. "I'll do it."

"Thank you," she said quietly. "You won't regret it."

He doubted that. "There's a condition."

She stiffened fractionally, then nodded.

"We have to live at my ranch for the year."

"Live...at your ranch," she repeated as if trying to comprehend a strange language.

"That's the condition."

The moonlight picked up the flash of her teeth as she smiled, then she laughed, a soft relieved flutter of merriment in the moon-glazed night.

"Well, what's your answer?" he demanded. Her laughter invaded his blood, causing it to froth and pop like champagne bubbling through his veins.

"I'll do it." She laughed again.

He wondered if he'd lost his mind.

## Chapter Two

Jessica moved without thinking. She closed the two steps between them and caught him by the shoulders. The next thing she knew, her hands were pinned over her head and she was flat against the wall. Brody held her captive between the wall and the warm cage of his body.

She blinked up at him in stunned surprise. She sensed the moment his reaction to her sudden move changed to one of sensual arousal. He released her and backed up.

"Sorry. You took me by surprise," he said gruffly.

"Me, too."

They stood there, only inches apart, their breaths quick and audible in the dark room. Awareness sizzled in the air between them. A strange lethargy filled her at the same time a whirlwind took control of her body. She swayed slightly and put out her hands for balance.

Brody steadied her with a hand on her arm. His fingertips brushed her breast as he did. She gasped. The whirlwind became a roar of wild yearning, bursting from someplace deeply hidden in the nooks and crannies of her soul.

"Brody?" she whispered, filled with wonder at the sensations that arced and glittered between them, surprised and enchanted as a sweet softness stole over her. She laid a hand on his chest.

His hands grasped her upper arms, and he held her when she would have moved into the warm shelter of his body. A low murmur of protest pushed its way from her throat.

"Don't," he said. His tone was harsh, like rocks being forced through a crusher.

"I'm sorry." She didn't know why she was apologizing. Her voice was husky with the desire that flooded her. They were a mere five feet from her bed, its whiteness a foil to the darkness that quivered and stirred with restless energy all around them.

It was strange...to find passion when she least expected it, to know it was there for them to share... She shivered as the magic washed over her, enchanting, beguiling, beckoning them to follow its sweet, wild call...

Brody muttered an expletive and thrust himself away. "You've bought yourself a husband, Ms. Lockhart, not a toy to be turned on at your bidding."

Brought abruptly back to earth, she watched while he locked the outside doors and left her room by the hall door. When he was gone, she wrapped her arms over her chest and felt the cold seep in. If it touched her heart, she would surely die.

* * *

Jessica heard Brody's deep voice conversing with her grandfather before she entered the breakfast room. She slowed, reluctant to face him. Chiding her sudden attack of nerves, she strode into the room with her head high.

Brody's eyes were on the door when she walked through. Although she wore ballet slippers and made no discernible sound as she walked, he'd somehow known she was there. His eyes swept over her as if surveying a mine field where hidden explosives lurked in every inch.

She felt as self-conscious as she had when at fourteen her breasts had swelled from bud to full bloom almost overnight. She smoothed the vibrant pink sweater over her hips and wished she'd worn a blouse instead of the clinging silk knit.

"Good morning, Jessica," her grandfather said in his usual somber way.

"Good morning." She gave Brody a cool glance. "Good morning, Brody." She selected toast and a poached egg.

"Coffee or tea?" Brody asked. He appeared beside her.

"Coffee."

He poured her a cup, then refilled his own and her grandfather's. They returned to the table. She ate while the men resumed their conversation about the storm that was supposed to hit that night. When there was a lull, she put down her fork.

Waiting until her grandfather had taken a sip of coffee and replaced the cup in the saucer, she asked, "Did Brody mention our news?"

A beat of silence followed the question.

"What news is that?" the older man asked. His dark eyebrows rose fractionally.

Jessica thought he was an incredibly handsome man to be sixty-six years old. Physically he looked twenty years younger. His hair was smooth and thick and pure silver. His high forehead gave him a patrician air.

Ronald Leary had been ten years younger than her grandmother, and everyone had been scandalized at the marriage of the wealthy widow to the younger attorney in her deceased husband's firm twenty-five years ago. However, he'd been a good husband, and the marriage had been stable.

As far as Jessica was concerned, he was her grandfather. He'd been there when her beloved grandmother had died, then her father, and finally her mother. If her life as the only child in his house during vacations from boarding school had been lonely, it wasn't his fault. He'd done his best for her.

Once he'd railed against her mother and the foolish conditions of the will. Jessica, shocked and hurt, had defended her mother. Seeing that he'd hurt Jessica with his harsh words, he'd never mentioned it again. For all those reasons and more, she felt a fierce loyalty toward him.

"Brody and I are to be married."

Her grandfather froze. He flushed deep red. A blood vessel enlarged and throbbed at each side of his neck. He laid a fisted hand on the table at each side of his plate. He leaned forward in the chair, his eyes on Brody.

"Pack up and get out," he said.

"Grandfather," she protested, shocked at this turn of events. "What are you saying?"

"How much will it cost to get rid of you?" he demanded of Brody, ignoring her.

Jessica had never heard him sound so harsh and contemptuous in her life. He looked ready to leap from his chair and kill Brody on the spot.

Brody leaned back in his chair as if thinking about it. "You don't have enough money," he finally said.

Jessica gasped. Brody flicked a glance her way, then studied her grandfather with insolent poise.

Her grandfather's flush deepened, and she worried about a stroke. "Please," she said, laying a hand on his sleeve.

He shook her off. "Be damned to that fancy lawyer who recommended you. I knew you were a fortune hunter the moment I saw you."

Brody's lips tilted up at the corners in that maddening little grin that wasn't a smile.

"Stop it," Jessica said, butting in to head off the escalating tension. She may as well have spit into the wind for all the good it did her. The men continued to scrutinize each other, her grandfather angry, Brody as cool as silk.

"Did you seduce her?" her grandfather continued, his eyes narrowing. "Is she pregnant?"

Brody didn't answer. Instead he gave the older man a stare that would have withered a strangler fig in ten seconds flat.

She stood up. That finally got their attention. "I am not going to sit here and be insulted and ignored. When either or both of you are ready to listen, I'll tell you my plans."

With her back ramrod straight, she sailed out of the dining room. Her legs trembled as she rushed down the hall. She was shocked at her grandfather's accusation.

She knew he was protective and all that, but to accuse Brody...

Pregnant, indeed. In her room, she curled into her favorite chair and propped her elbow on the padded arm. She covered her eyes with her hand. So much for her big announcement.

The door opened. She wasn't startled when Brody walked in unannounced. She kept a wary eye on him.

"When do you want to set the date?" he asked. He shoved his hands into his pockets and leaned against the door. They could have been discussing an appointment for the dentist.

"As soon as possible."

He nodded. "I can be packed and ready to leave in an hour. We can marry in Denver and get to the ranch before the blizzard breaks." He smiled. It transformed his face into a work of near beauty, but not quite. He was a man who'd lived hard in the world, too hard for something so simple as beauty.

She laid a hand over her aching heart. "It's Saturday."

His smile chilled. "We can fly to Vegas for the ceremony, then head out. I assume we aren't planning on having a society wedding with all the trimmings?"

"No."

"Good. How soon can you be ready to go?"

"An hour." She rose. There was one thing she wanted to know. "Uh, about the marriage. What besides the money are you expecting from it?"

He reached for the doorknob. "No entanglements," he said in a low, ominous tone, his face darkening.

That, she assumed, meant no intimacy. To her chagrin, she didn't know if she was hurt or relieved. She recalled his warmth surrounding her when he'd held her pinned to the wall. Winters were long and cold in Colorado, she'd heard.

She nodded.

He continued to gaze at her, his eyes like deep, dark pits filled with danger and secrets too dire for her to know. A shiver plunged down her spine. For a moment, she knew real fear. It rushed over her, causing her to draw back. Then she relaxed.

Brody was danger personified, but she trusted him with her life. She didn't know why.

Finally, with a satisfied air, he walked out.

As if freed from a spell, she dashed to her closet and set out her luggage. In fifty-one minutes, she had her clothes rolled and packed with underwear, gloves and scarves tucked into the middle the way she'd learned at school. She closed and locked the last piece, then opened the door to wait for Brody.

He appeared as the clock struck the hour. His dark eyes took in her three pieces of luggage and the weekend case that held her makeup and toiletries. He nodded, as grim as a funeral attendee. Their wedding generated no joy for him.

Her grandfather met them in the foyer. "You're foolish to do this," he said. His color was nearly normal, except for the twin flags of anger that highlighted his cheekbones.

"I have to." She realized she did.

He touched her shoulder, a thing he rarely did. Expressions of affection didn't come easily to him. She hugged him, feeling the fierceness of love churn in her, then stepped back before she embarrassed both of them with tears.

"The car is here," Brody said. His hand propelled her toward the door.

She looked back as they left the house. Her grand-father stood where she'd left him, his hands clenched into fists. The harshness of his expression frightened her. Hatred gleamed in his eyes as he stared at Brody.

It was an inauspicious note on which to begin a new life.

In the car, Brody handed her a handkerchief without speaking. She wiped her eyes, leaving a dark smudge of mascara on the white cotton. Brody took the hand-kerchief and stuck it into his pocket when she finished.

The wind at the airport chilled her to the bone. While Brody checked their bags, the driver paused by her. "We'll miss you, Miss Jessica, the missus and I." He tipped his hat and left them. She watched the taillights disappear.

A hand touched her shoulder. "It's time."

She looked up, her thoughts in a whirl. She wanted to chase after the car and return home where she knew who she was and what would happen the next day and the next...

Brody's midnight gaze shot questions at her. She realized he thought she would change her mind, that he'd expected it all along. She lifted her chin.

"Yes. I'm ready."

The wind shifted and hit them full force. The shiny strands of Brody's hair caught the sun as they lifted and settled across his forehead. His breath huffed out frostily, as if he sighed.

He slipped an arm around her shoulders. "Come," he said. The tone was oddly gentle.

Brody slipped the ring on his bride's icy finger. She'd seemed in a daze since they'd left her home that

morning. It was early afternoon. Flying west, they'd
gained an hour.

They signed the papers that made them officially
husband and wife. Leaving the wedding parlor, they
walked out into seventy-degree heat. "Do you want to
spend the night and fly in tomorrow?"

She shook her head.

The cab was waiting. They returned to the airport.
In an hour, they were on their way north. They landed
in Denver well before dark. His sports utility vehicle,
with its necessary four-wheel drive, was at his office.
They took a cab downtown.

"Is it far?" she asked, practically her first sentence
in the past six hours.

"An hour's drive." He helped the driver move their
bags from the cab to the rear of the sports ute.

After the cab left, he frowned at his wife. She stood
there in the lengthening shadows of the parking lot, her
gaze on the lofty white peaks that formed a backdrop
to Denver's skyscrapers.

Her gray eyes reflected the lavender shades of twilight. He recognized sadness and a longing for things
he couldn't describe in those translucent depths. She
squared her shoulders as if facing off against the world.
"Shall we go?"

He was reminded of the boy he'd once been, lost
and abandoned and frightened...and determined that no
one would know it. He cleared his throat. "Yeah."

"Tell me about your ranch. Is that where you live
when you're not out solving cases?" she asked when
they were on their way out of town.

The highway was clear. He punched on the cruise
control. The act of driving gave him something to concentrate on and he regained his equilibrium. Jessica

Lockhart...Smith, he corrected, wasn't anything like the boy he'd once been.

She'd simply seen a way out of her dilemma and had grabbed it. For himself, he'd get a nice bundle of cash out of the deal. That's all he wanted and was as far as he'd involve himself. Except for keeping her safe for the year.

Jessica had trouble keeping her eyes open. They were passing through a small town tucked up in a mountain valley above Denver. The town drifted behind them. The road narrowed into a winding county highway. She didn't know where they were. She realized she didn't care. Being with Brody was enough at the moment. She felt safe...

"We're here."

She sat up and peered through the deep twilight. A ranch house was barely visible among a stand of tall trees. It appeared to be made of timber and stone. "Is this your home?"

"Yes." He shoved open the door. Cold air rushed into the sports ute. Brody handed her the weekend case when she hopped out to help him with the luggage. "I'll get the rest."

She followed him up the snow-dusted flagstones to the house. Shivers raced along her back. Her legs trembled. She couldn't decide what she was afraid of.

Not Brody. That much she knew.

Inside, he set her luggage in a stone foyer, then turned the thermostat up. She heard the stir of air, then felt it cascade onto her shoulders from a vent overhead. Her mouth dried up like a desert lake when he started forward again.

He handled her three large cases with ease, reminding her of how strong he was. He led her to a bedroom tucked under the stairs. A sturdy oak bed angled out from the corner rather than being set against the wall. A cedar chest was conveniently located at the foot of the bed. A rocking chair and table occupied another corner. A corner cabinet was filled with books and a dried arrangement of leaves and grasses in a huge snifter.

"The bathroom is through that door," Brody informed her. "There's a walk-in closet here." He placed her luggage in front of the chest, then opened doors.

The bed was larger than standard. She thought of them in it, of his arms around her, holding her close. No one had hugged her since her mother had died.

"Is this your room?" she asked, letting herself look at him, this silent, scowling man who was her husband. *Husband.*

The word astonished her. An unbearable lightness stole over her, a mist of longing for the life that eluded her.

"It's yours." He strode to the door. "For a year." He walked out without a backward glance.

She sat on the bed and rubbed a hand over the old-fashioned quilt. She wondered if she dared invite him to share it. With that thought haunting her, she unpacked her nightgown, washed up and went to sleep almost immediately.

The blizzard had struck during the night, silently dumping its load of snow over the landscape while she slept. She dressed in wool slacks and an oversize sweater of Nordic design in blue and white. In thick sports socks, she padded into the main quarters of the ranch house.

The living room and kitchen were modern in creature comforts, but rustic in tone. The outer wall was made from twelve-inch logs that were square cut, the caulking painted white. A stone fireplace separated the living room from the kitchen-family room. She walked into the kitchen.

A half pot of coffee awaited her on the kitchen counter. She poured a cup and glanced out the window.

Her heart skipped around in her chest when she spotted a bundled figure out in a paddock. The errant organ righted itself with a dull thud when she realized the man wasn't Brody, but someone shorter and thinner. The man was checking the sheep in the pasture.

Laughter bubbled out of her when she spotted the llamas on the far side of the barn. They were watching the man with expressions of avid curiosity. Occasionally they glanced at each other and nodded as if approving his actions.

She ate two pieces of toast with peanut butter and jelly before donning boots and the fox fur and heading outside.

Standing at the end of the porch leading off from the kitchen, her breath caught at the beauty around her. The sky was the incredible blue of postcards, the snow so white it hurt her eyes. A row of jagged mountain peaks rose to the north of the house, awesome in their grandeur.

Closer to the house was a ridge of rimrock that slanted upward at a thirty degree angle, ending in a fifty-foot cliff. When the snow cleared, she'd hike up there.

From the porch, tracks sank deep into the fresh snow. Brody. She wondered how long he'd been up and where he was.

After another minute of indecision, she plunged into the snow, stretching her steps to match his. Although he was a bit under six feet tall, he had a long stride. She had to leap from one print to another. All went well for about half the distance to the barn, then she caught her toe on an unseen object and fell facedown into a fluffy drift.

She floundered helplessly in the soft, dry powder. The more she fought to sit up, the deeper she sank. When she opened her eyes, she could see nothing but snow. It surrounded her, filling her mouth and nose, stinging her eyes as she tried to fight her way out. It pressed upon her from top and bottom, from every side as well.

When she realized she couldn't tell which way was up, panic set in. She quickly quelled it. Lying still, she cleared a space in front of her nose with her gloved hand. The snow caved in. She cupped both hands in front of her face to maintain a breathing hole.

Her breath sounded loud in the confined space, and the air seemed thin. If only she'd yelled a greeting to the shepherd, he might have come to her aid. As it was, no one knew she was in trouble. She might be trapped until the snow melted.

Stop it, she chided her runaway imagination. She surely wasn't going to suffocate right there in the yard, less than a hundred feet from the house. She merely had to get her bearings.

When she'd fallen, she'd gone in headfirst. She was pretty sure she'd slithered down an embankment of some kind, but not a terribly deep one. She'd once read that if she was caught in an avalanche, she should swim. It seemed silly, but she'd try it.

With the weight of the snow all around her, she

found she couldn't swim, but she could make a crawling motion rather like a clumsy frog. Dizziness washed over her. The panic edged closer.

She paused and listened. The silence was absolute. Being under the snow was like being underwater. The snow crept around her face and down her neck. The cold seeped into her. It was, she found, very peaceful—

Something grasped her foot in talons of iron. She started, then struggled for all she was worth against the monster that was dragging her deeper into the snow. Panic took over.

The next moment was a confused swirl of snow and fox fur as her coat slid past her. *Avalanche.* She flailed as hard as she could. Swim, she ordered her frozen limbs.

"Be still, dammit," a growly masculine voice ordered.

Suddenly the world reappeared through a haze of fur and falling snow, blinding sunlight and dark eyes that snapped with fury. Brody let go her leg and caught her under her arms. The world whirled again, then righted itself as Brody stood and she was set on her feet.

Rough hands brushed snow off her face and settled her coat over her body after giving it a good shake.

She laid her hands on his arms to steady herself. She grinned, knowing she looked foolish, but unable to help it. "Good morning," she said.

"Have you lost your mind? Only fools wander around in the snow when they don't know the lay of the land."

"I guess that puts me in my place." She grinned some more, so happy to see him she wanted to give him a kiss. In fact, that sounded like a fine idea. She grabbed the lapels of his plaid wool jacket and planted one on his jaw, missing his mouth by a quarter inch. When she would have tried again, he held her off.

"I wanted to thank you," she explained. "I thought I was going to suffocate."

He was unrelenting. "You should have." He looped an arm around her and propelled her to the porch. He lifted her easily and set her down on the top step. "Stay inside. I don't have time to chase after you like a Saint Bernard dashing to the rescue every time you get a fool notion in your head."

"Have you had breakfast?"

The change of subject caused him to blink. "No."

"That's why you're so grouchy," she concluded. "I was coming to ask what time you'd be at the house. Do you like eggs *en papillote?*"

"No."

"You don't know what they are. You'll love them. I can make gravy, too."

"I won't be coming in. Don and I have work to do."

"Don?"

"Don Adono. He works for me."

"The shepherd I saw in the pasture earlier?"

"Yeah. Lucky for you he saw you fall in the dip. A creek runs through here in the spring." He gestured to the place where she'd fallen in.

"Why didn't you fall?"

"I knew it was there. I jumped across."

"No wonder that step was so long. I was wondering how to manage it when I stumbled over something."

"There're rocks along the sides of the creek. Stay put." He walked off.

"Wait. When will you be in?"

He turned and watched her for a long second. She

put a hand up to her hair self-consciously and felt the snow clinging to the strands. She noticed the snow on him. If she had as much snow on her as he had on him, and she was sure she did, they must look like the fabled abominable snowmen in person.

She leaned forward and brushed the snow off his lapels. "I thought I was in an avalanche. When you yanked me out by my ankle," she added at his ominous frown. "I thought...well, never mind... Thanks for coming to the rescue." She patted him on the cheek. "Breakfast in half an hour."

Leaving him standing on the steps, she retreated gracefully into the house, then flew around hanging up her coat and tugging off her boots. She quickly combed her hair into order with her fingers and shook off the last of the snow.

Her cheeks flamed with cold and excitement. She paused to look at the plain gold band on her left hand. This was her first morning as a wife. And what a start.

With a laugh, she checked out the refrigerator and pantry. She decided on sausage and eggs scrambled with green peppers and onions, cottage-fried potatoes and hot flour tortillas. With a jar of salsa to go with the meal, she had it ready in thirty minutes. Forty-five minutes later, she admitted Brody wasn't going to come in.

She propped her chin on her hands and thought the situation over. She wanted to make this year easy on both of them. She'd be a wife if it killed her...or him.

## Chapter Three

The door opened. Jessica watched in pleased surprise as a bulky figure entered the kitchen. Another, smaller male followed Brody inside. The men took off their gloves, coats and hats, then washed up at the utility sink in the corner. Brody didn't offer to introduce her or the other man.

She had a hard time tearing her gaze from her husband. He was dressed in jeans and a flannel shirt. He wore blue waffle-knit underwear, visible at the neck, under the flannel. A glow produced by the cold permeated his dusky skin. The freshness of the outdoors clung to his broad shoulders. She'd never seen him look so vibrant, so alive and virile. She swallowed and forced her attention to the older man.

"Good morning. You must be Don Adono. Brody has spoken of you. I'm Jessica." She glanced at Brody, then tilted her chin up. "Jessica Smith, Brody's wife."

The shepherd was one of those men whose age was impossible to determine. His days in the sun had given him a weather-beaten appearance, but his wiry frame and movements indicated strength and agility. His hair had some gray sprinkled through it, but not copiously. He was close to her grandfather's age, she decided, going by the lines on his face.

"Pleased to meet you," the shepherd replied with old-fashioned courtesy. He smiled and bobbed his head.

Hmm, her husband could take some lessons in manners from his hired hand. He had yet to offer her a greeting.

"Thank you. I'll get your breakfast. Do be seated, gentlemen." She glanced at Brody when he came to the table.

His expression was not encouraging. He took a chair and watched without a word while she took the bowls from the oven and placed them on stone squares she'd found on a shelf. The squares must have been left over from those in the entry hall since they were the same design.

She tried not to watch him as if she were a neophyte trying to please her master while he sampled her cooking. Instead she rolled a tortilla around the scrambled eggs and spooned some salsa over it. Don put everything, including the sausage and potatoes, inside the tortilla, wrapped it up and, holding it in his hands, ate it with quick, neat bites. Brody did the same.

After finishing, Jessica watched in amazement as the men ate three servings each, cleaning out every bowl. She thought they would have eaten more if she'd prepared it.

"Verra good," Don said, displaying a slight accent.

She asked him where he was from originally.

"I was born here, but my parents were Basque."

"How interesting. Were they from the French or Spanish side of the mountains?"

"Spanish."

Brody's eyes flicked to her in surprise when, in Spanish, she asked Don what other languages he spoke. She and the shepherd discussed the Basque region and the number of Basque families now living in the States. Don had relatives in California, a sister and her husband plus two nieces and three nephews. His two brothers and their wives and children lived on the family ranch in southern Colorado.

She switched back to English so Brody wouldn't feel left out. "I always wanted brothers and sisters. I felt I'd missed so much by not having a large family. Did you feel that way?" she asked her husband.

"No."

The blunt answer momentarily halted the conversation. "But you had a foster sister, didn't you? That must have been nice. Does she have a family?"

He nodded, then sipped his coffee. The furnace clicked off. The silence eddied around them. Deciding to use it to advantage, she smiled sweetly and waited.

"Carly lives on a ranch in northern California," he finally said. "Her husband has a son by a former marriage who lives with them. They're expecting a child later this year."

Jessica thought of having children. Hers and Brody's? He'd probably have a coronary if she mentioned wanting a child. But a baby... The idea grabbed her and wouldn't let go. She wondered what kind of father he'd make.

Was there nurturing or tenderness in this tough hombre she'd married? She doubted she would ever know. That caused an odd hurting twist inside. She pushed aside the useless thoughts.

"Could I speak to you?" she asked politely when the men rose to leave.

He scowled impatiently. "I'll meet you at the stable," he told the shepherd.

After the older man left, Jessica refilled hers and Brody's coffee cups, then resumed her seat. "I need to know the setup here. Shall I do the cooking and take care of the house while you do outside chores, or do you prefer another arrangement?"

Something like amazement stormed through his dark eyes, then his mouth moved slightly in a cynical snarl. "What do you know about taking care of a house?"

"I can do it." She waited.

He studied her for a tense thirty seconds. "I have a woman from a neighboring ranch come in twice a month. She cleans, changes the beds and washes the clothes. Don and I do our own cooking and cleaning in the meantime."

She nodded. "I'll do the cooking and keep the place picked up during the week. Do you need me to do anything outside?"

"Like what?"

"I can ride. I've been on a cattle drive—"

"At a dude ranch, on vacation?"

She quelled her rising temper at his contemptuous manner. "I spent several summers with a friend whose family owned a ranch. A working ranch," she added for good measure. "I can pull calves, brand, open gates, whatever is necessary."

"I'm impressed." He stood and put his hat, gloves and coat on. "Just stay out of the way and out of trouble. I don't have time to watch you every second. The ewes will start dropping their lambs any day. Blizzards are one of their favorite times. Like most females, they like to make life as hard as possible.''

She flung her napkin on her plate and stood, the chair screeching on the vinyl-coated wood flooring. "You're getting paid a damn good salary and bonus to watch me every second."

The next thing she knew, he was in her face, a handful of sweater gathered into a big fist that rested under her chin. "I'll make sure you're safe," he told her with an icy snarl, "but nobody owns me. You got that?"

She returned his hateful stare without a blink. "Loud and clear. If we're going to make it through a year without serious words between us, we'd better come to some agreement about what we expect from each other."

He relaxed his hold and stepped away. "I expect you to do what I tell you. I expect you to stay out of the way and not interfere with work the way you did today."

"Stay out of the way. Don't interfere." She crossed her arms and tapped her fingers. "I can handle that." She paused for emphasis. "But don't tell me what to do, Brody."

"I knew there was a reason I shouldn't take on this job. Are we going to fight over every single thing?"

"I don't know. Are we?" She sent the verbal ball back to his court.

His eyes narrowed, but that was all the emotion he displayed. He walked out, giving the door a solid slam behind him. She watched him cross the yard and jump the gully she'd fallen into. Someday she'd find out what, besides passion, lay beneath that tough exterior.

* * *

Jessica yawned, then stared at the ceiling. The bed was warm. She hated to get up. She wasn't a morning person, but she'd learned to rise early during her years abroad. Now she woke up at six even though she'd stayed awake reading until midnight the previous evening.

She'd left a pot of stew on the stove and gone to her room at ten. Brody hadn't come in until very late. She wondered if he'd watched from the barn until she'd turned off the light in her bedroom. She'd heard him upstairs in the shower soon after he'd arrived. Later, she'd listened as he came down the stairs and entered the kitchen. He'd paused outside her door before going to his room for the night.

Don Adono had a house of his own. She'd seen him go to it and lights come on when she'd been peeling vegetables for the stew. She wondered if Brody had eaten lunch at Don's house.

She sighed and watched the snow hit the windows of the cozy bedroom. They hadn't had but one day's respite from the blizzard. The news last night had included a weather alert. The state police had asked that everyone keep off the roads until the storm let up and they could clear the highways.

The wind whistled around the eaves of the snug house. March was supposed to be windy, but it was the last day of the month. In like a lion, out like a lamb. That was the saying.

Brody roared like a lion...well, he acted fierce, but maybe his heart was gentle. If anyone could reach it.

She blinked the sleep from her eyes, startled at the direction of her thoughts. She had only a year. That probably wasn't enough time to dig through the layers of granite Brody had encased himself in.

Sluggish, she pushed the covers off and shivered as the cooler air of the room hit her. Maybe she should start sleeping in a sweat suit. She hurried to the shower.

When she entered the kitchen, she gave a start at finding Brody at the table, a coffee cup in his hand. He was scowling at the blizzard howling outside the window.

The temperature on the back porch was eighteen degrees, a drop of ten degrees from the night before. "Cold," she commented. "What are your plans for the day?"

"Staying warm and hoping the sheep don't drop any more lambs until the storm is over." He gave her one cursory glance, then went back to eyeing the storm.

"Do they usually have them in March?"

"Only if there's a blizzard." He sounded as if he thought the ewes planned the births to inconvenience him.

She smiled at his exasperation. It almost made him seem human. "Did you get the pregnant ewes in the barn?"

"Hardly. We have a thousand head."

"Oh. Are all of them expecting?"

"About eighty percent."

"I noticed a dozen llamas in one paddock. Are they expecting, too?"

"Three of the older females are."

"What are you doing with them?"

He turned his dark gaze on her, causing little tendrils of electricity to arc through her. "I'm thinking of establishing a herd for wool."

She nodded in understanding. "I've heard their fur

is some of the warmest in the world. Are you going to have ski clothes made from the wool?''

"No, work clothes for ranchers who have to drag lambs out of blizzards to keep them from freezing to death.''

"That makes sense,'' she said agreeably. She mixed up a batch of biscuits and put them in the oven. "Do you like fried eggs?'' She cracked one into the pan for herself. When he didn't answer, she gave him an inquiring glance.

Brody thought his blood was going to boil. Jessica wasn't wearing a bra under the sweat suit. Her breasts bounced in an unbounded way with each move she made. She had to know she was driving him crazy. He needed to touch her, to know the smooth heat of her skin once more...

He cursed silently and gripped the cup with an unsteady hand. He and Don had been up half the night taking care of lambs and ewes, now he had to face *her* when he was tired and his defenses were down.

He risked a glance at her perfectly shaped rear as she bent over to check the biscuits. She'd made the damn things from scratch. He'd seen it with his own eyes. He hadn't known she knew which end of a skillet went on the stove.

Muscles rippled jauntily at him when she straightened. He wanted to walk over to her and take her right there, maybe sitting on the counter, his body snug in hers...

He suppressed a groan and forced his attention back to the storm. He tried to figure out why he'd thought it was a good idea to get her here before the storm broke. Oh, yeah, so nothing would happen to her if her brakes went out on a slick road back at her home. The storm was supposed to blanket the entire northern part of the country.

Gazing out the window, he thought nature was doing its best to comply with the weather forecast. He rubbed a weary hand over his face.

"Breakfast."

Something wonderful wafted below his nose. He removed his hand and stared at eggs cooked to perfection, two slices of ham browned just right, biscuits that looked as if they'd float right off the plate and a steaming bowl of gravy.

If that wasn't enough to drive a man wild, her scent floated around him as she reached past him to refresh his coffee cup. She used lavender-scented soap and shampoo, he recalled, that matched her perfume.

"Look," he said, almost in desperation. "You don't have to do the housewife act."

"Why not?" She sounded insolent.

"Because you're not a wife." He tried to lighten up. "I don't want to get used to this, then have it stop when you get tired of playing house."

"I am your wife." She gave him a level perusal, then went to the phone. "Shall I call Don and see if he wants to come over?"

"He's already eaten by now."

She nodded and prepared a plate for herself. When she joined him at the table, he realized she wore thick socks but no shoes. It made her seem more approachable, more like plain Jessica Smith and not Jessica Lacey Lockhart of the Virginia Laceys and the Chicago Lockharts.

The food was perfect, but he couldn't concentrate on it. He was too aware of the woman next to him and the fact...the awesome fact...that she was his wife.

For one year.

That was something else he didn't intend to forget. He wasn't going to get used to having her around. *I love you, hon, but I got to go.* He knew about women. His own mom hadn't been able to stick around.

He'd learned early, after his father had left them, then his mother had opted out, not to trust anyone with his whole heart. It only got in the way when it was time to move on.

He broke open a biscuit and watched the steam rise and disappear. He ladled gravy over the halves, then took a bite. Ambrosia. It was the best meal he'd ever eaten. Except for the stew and hot bread ready in the oven when he got in late last night. That had warmed his insides as no fire ever could.

Something else that could warm a man was a passionate woman waiting for him in bed.

Frowning at the woman who quietly ate her breakfast as she contemplated the snow that fell steadily outside the windows, he felt danger closing in. A man could get in over his head before he knew it with a woman like her.

On the surface, she seemed to be the answer to a lonely man's dreams. He knew her for the socialite she was. Charity work was a way for rich people to feel good about themselves, meet for lunch at expensive restaurants and get their pictures in the paper. He'd seen it all before.

He'd almost fallen for one of his client's daughters. Until he'd mentioned marriage in a casual way. She'd made it plain he was great for fun and games, but not up to her social register when it came to bloodlines.

He could handle that as long as he knew where he stood.

The trouble with Jessica was he didn't know any such thing. She didn't act the way she was supposed to. He'd thought she'd want to head right back to Chicago when she saw his home and the wilderness surrounding the ranch. She hadn't said a word about the isolation or lack of servants. Instead she'd pitched in without being asked. It made him uneasy.

"Why the big frown? Aren't the eggs to your liking?"

He refocused his thoughts. "They're fine." He paused. "The biscuits are good, too. Everything is."

"But?"

"I just wonder how long it's going to last." He gave her an assessing glance. She'd last a week at the outside.

"For a year?" she suggested, that one slender brow, the one with an attitude, going up slightly, mocking his doubts.

Mocking? No, by damn, she was challenging him.

"We'll see," he said.

She smiled and didn't say a word.

Brody hit the window frame with the flat of his hand. The blizzard showed no signs of abating. The weather had been fitful for five days with no clearing in sight. It was one of the worst storms in recorded history. One side of the cabin was buried in drifts to the porch rafters.

From the second-floor bedroom where he was sleeping—or not sleeping, as the case may be—he could see Don dropping hay off the flatbed for the cattle.

They'd spent the morning collecting ewes and lambs and bringing them in to the inner paddock. They'd built a storm shelter with bales of hay set at ninety-degree angles to the barn and used the tractor scoop to keep the area relatively clear of snow. He wondered how many lambs and calves he'd lose this year.

His salary and bonus would cover the loss. He frowned. Jessica's money. He hadn't gotten to the bank to deposit the check for the first month yet.

Going to his desk, he looked at the amount and her signature at the bottom. The other trustees had been dismayed when she'd called and told them she was married. When the storm was over, he planned to forward a certified copy of their marriage license so they and her grandfather would know the marriage was for real.

He'd wondered if either of the three could be in on the attempts on her life when he'd taken the case. A discreet check had disclosed no skulduggery. An audit of the books had proven her money was wisely invested and carefully guarded.

Still, he had a gut feeling that all was not as it appeared on the surface. As Jessica's husband, he had more leeway to follow his instincts. He'd hired his own investigator to check into a few details he was interested in.

Her uncle, for one. The man seemed to have recouped his losses from prior bad investments and appeared to be doing well.

Brody had learned never to go by appearances.

Then there was the grandfather. The old man had nearly had apoplexy when he'd learned of the marriage. Strange that all his attention had been focused on the groom and not the bride. Odd, too, was the fact that her grandfather had managed to isolate a woman of her charm from most eligible males, thus ensuring her single state. Were the two men conspiring to keep her fortune for themselves?

A grim smile crimped the corners of his mouth. Little did they know, to paraphrase an old novel he'd once read, that the marriage could be annulled quite honestly and legally.

A tightening in his nether regions reminded him that this chaste state of affairs was not to his body's liking. Damn, he was having erotic dreams every night as if he were a pubescent teenager with hormone surges.

From his open door, he detected signs of life below. Turning from the storm, he went downstairs to see what his wife would cook for breakfast this morning. Yesterday it had been whole-wheat pancakes, so delicate he'd hardly had to chew.

Don had taken to coming over and having the midday meal with them. Jessica always sent him home with enough food for his supper, too. She'd cooked a roast on Monday and prepared different dishes from it all week. When the housekeeper hadn't been able to get over, she'd cleaned house, too.

However, she'd asked before going into his room. Feeling guilty, he'd cleaned it himself and washed the sheets and the stack of towels accumulating in the bathroom. She'd made up the bed with fresh sheets, though, and left a lingering trace of her lavender-based perfume to haunt him every minute he was there.

Entering the kitchen, he saw Jessica with a cookbook in hand, leafing through the recipes. "Run out of ideas?"

She glanced up, her gray eyes as beautiful as a cat's, hazy with the misty translucence of rain seen across a great distance.

They unnerved him, those eyes. They seemed to

gaze at some point far beyond the horizon, seeking things that no mere mortal could see. Sometimes he wanted to ask what she sought when she stood gazing out the window at the mountains.

He didn't. She'd probably think he was a fool.

"No, just browsing."

"What smells so good?"

"Oatmeal."

"Oh."

Her smile switched from warm and sexy to teasing. "Yes, Oliver, you may have a second bowl."

"Of oatmeal? No, thanks."

"You'll eat those words. Don is going to join us. I thought you both could use something that would warm you up and stick to your ribs after being out in that weather."

"It's zero today," he commented, recalling the harsh bite of the cold through thermal underwear, jeans and waterproof pants.

She made clicking sounds of disapproval and proceeded to set the table. His mouth actually watered when she set a bowl of the porridge in front of him. It smelled of cinnamon and spices he couldn't identify. Butter floated on top along with caramelized brown sugar. A loaf of cinnamon bread came out of the oven. She wrapped it in a towel and set it in a wooden bowl before placing it and a bread knife on the table.

"Eat up before it gets cold," she advised. She poured a pitcher of milk and brought it to him.

The scent of lavender wafted around him along with the cinnamon and oatmeal. Her hip brushed his arm as she set the small pitcher down. Without thinking, he reached out.

His hand settled on her waist and slid along the enticing curve of her hip. He was aware of her in every clamoring cell of his body. He needed more than food for sustenance.

She put a hand on his shoulder as if she needed support, then she slipped her fingers under his hair, which had grown to collar length, and caressed the back of his neck.

Heat like a flash fever ran through him.

When she made no move to run from him, he let his hand glide along her thigh. Again she wore a sweat suit, this time in a forest green with leaves embroidered on the front. Again she wore no bra, but he'd felt the line of her underwear high on her leg. He moved his hand under the shirt and up to her back.

As smooth as silk, with no strap crossing the slender expanse of her rib cage.

He swallowed. His mouth dried up as if dusted with bonemeal. He couldn't dislodge the knot that had formed in his throat. Or the ridge that bloomed in the sweats he'd changed into when he'd returned to the house.

Glancing up, he found her gaze on his arousal. Her face took on a thoughtful mien. He wondered how far she'd let him go before she demanded he stop.

"I had wondered if sex was to be a part of our bargain," she said, her voice as soft as a whisper.

It shocked him into action. He jerked his hand away from her warmth and out of her shirt. He couldn't believe he'd lost himself that way, forgetting everything but the feel of her.

"No." His voice came out a growl of anger.

"I think…" She gazed past him out the window, then back at him. "I think I wouldn't mind."

Blood surged through him in so many places at once,

he couldn't respond for a second. When he could get his bearings in a world gone crazy, it was too late. Don was on the porch, stomping snow off his boots before he came in.

Jessica went to the counter and poured another cup of coffee. "I was afraid we were going to have to come rescue you. You must be frozen by now."

The old shepherd grinned in his bashful way as he hung up his outer clothing, then took the place set for him.

Brody realized his seemingly guileless wife had enchanted his hired hand just as much as she had him a moment ago. He'd be on his guard against such foolishness in the future.

After the delicious meal, he and Don went out to check the ewes once more. They cleared snow and left it piled up for a windbreak against the fence. Any protection was better than none from the fierce wind that beat down from the northwest.

It was four o'clock and already as dark as twilight when he entered the house again. A fire crackled in the stone fireplace in the living room. His wife was asleep on the sofa.

He sat on the floor and removed his insulated boots, then set them on the hearth to dry. He stretched his toes toward the flames. Ah, that felt good. It was the first time his feet had been warm in hours.

He leaned against the sofa. Behind him, Jessica turned to her side. Her hand dangled over his shoulder. He risked a glance at her. Sound asleep.

Stuffing a floor pillow behind him, he let his head rest on the sofa. In a minute, he felt a caress on his neck.

She continued to rub lightly along his neck and collarbone until he sighed and closed his eyes. He didn't know when her hand stilled. He went to sleep.

Jessica woke reluctantly. Her dream was of summer fields dotted with wildflowers and shady pine woods. She breathed deeply and inhaled the scent of balsam and subtle spice. Instinctively she pushed closer to the wonderful aroma and felt crisp strands of hair shift over her face.

Opening her eyes, she realized it was Brody's hair that had made her dream of piney woods and fields of fresh flowers. He smelled of shampoo and aftershave and an enticing masculine warmth that sent waves of heat shimmering through her.

She snuggled closer and let herself drift, a strange happiness suffusing her. Or maybe it was contentment. Whatever it was, she'd never felt it before.

With careful movements, she smoothed the strands of black hair off his forehead. He had nicely shaped ears, set close to his head, the rim a smooth arch ending in a thin lobe. She drew a finger around the edge and noticed he'd once had his left earlobe pierced.

That small fact seemed intimate, as if she'd discovered a wonderful secret about him that only she knew. If they had been really married, as in heart and soul married, what hopes and wishes would they confide in the quiet of their bedroom, perhaps after making love?

She would never know those things with Brody, not in their year together. During the few weeks he'd taken over her life, she'd learned practically nothing of his. She'd been stunned that he'd made living at the ranch a condition of the marriage.

However, she could see why he had wanted to come home. It was the most beautiful place she'd ever been.

There was something wild but peaceful about the mountains and this secure valley tucked in a fold between the hills. It made her heart soar, and for the first time as an adult, she felt a freedom she'd never had.

Brody had given this gift to her, this freedom to soar—

He turned his head, and she realized he was awake. In the dying embers of the fire, with no lights on in the house, his eyes seemed fathomless. They invited her to come to him...

A sensation rather like pain arced through her breasts. Her nipples beaded beneath the fleeced cotton of her sweat top.

She stopped stroking the silky strands of his hair and dropped her hand to the sofa, self-conscious at being caught touching him. He'd made it plain he was off limits.

He pushed himself to a sitting position and tossed the floor pillow aside. Electric currents ran over her nerves. He was watching her with such an odd expression, one almost of dislike, but with an intensity that drew her in like a netted butterfly. She couldn't look away.

Slowly his head came down. She realized he was going to kiss her. Her pulse pounded wildly, and her breath became trapped in her throat. She swallowed painfully.

Brody tilted his head slightly to the side, questioning her and what was happening. She didn't look away.

Letting his mouth settle lightly on hers, he flicked out his tongue and followed the outline of her lips. He'd been wanting to do that for days, he vaguely realized. He also knew his guard was down. He didn't care.

Her lips moved under his, and he felt her draw in a shaky breath before she pressed forward ever so little, enough to indicate she wanted more. Elation swept through him like champagne on an empty stomach.

He touched her shoulder. Part of him marveled at the delicacy of bone and tissue that composed this woman.

His wife.

The title still seemed odd to him, as odd as the one of husband. He couldn't relate it to himself or marriage to them.

Something savage rose up to remind him it wasn't a marriage in any sense of the word. He'd been a convenience to an heiress, a means to an end with her freedom from a will that had put her in danger the ultimate goal. He'd better remember that.

Her tongue touched his. He stiffened as fire shot through him in places he'd thought had shriveled and died years ago. Her touch brought them to painful, throbbing life.

"Brody," she whispered, an urgent sound of need that burned all thoughts from his head. She pressed against him.

Those breasts, those wonderful bouncy breasts that had teased and irritated him for weeks, knocked the breath out of him with just a touch. Closing his eyes to reason and self-preservation, he gathered her in and kissed her as if there was no tomorrow.

His hands, freed of restraint, slipped under the forest green top and stroked over skin so satiny smooth, it was like touching warm butter. Making a space between them, he glided up her rib cage and found the treasure.

Holding her was like holding a moonbeam that had

come to life. She was life and heat and every whimsy he'd ever had. When her breast beaded under his touch, he groaned and pulled back slightly. He had to see her, to enjoy fully this feast of the senses...now...before he woke...

Jessica almost sobbed as pleasure spiraled deep into the center of her being. Being kissed and held and caressed by Brody was the most wonderful thing she'd ever experienced. When he pushed her top up and his mouth closed over her breast, she almost cried out.

His tongue circled the engorged tip. His hands roamed over her at will. She slipped her hands under his sweats and caressed the smooth skin of his back. A shudder went through him.

He jerked his head up. "What the hell are we doing?"

"Making love?" she ventured, all her certainty fleeing as a dark scowl settled over his face.

"Entanglements," he stated. He pushed her hands off him and stood. "I'm not one of your toys, Jessica, to be picked up or laid aside at your pleasure. If you play the seductress, you'll pay the consequences."

She smoothed her top down. "What are they?"

He glared at her as if she'd cheated on some rules that only he knew. Then he walked out.

She heard his feet hitting the steps up to his room, then the firm closing of the door. She lay there and thought about being his wife while the fire in the hearth and the passion inside her slowly turned to ash.

## Chapter Four

Jessica jumped when the phone rang. Other than a couple of calls from her trustees after she'd informed them of her marriage, no one had called. She knew Brody had a phone in his bedroom office with a private line and that he used it to communicate with his office in Denver.

A few times during the week, she'd heard the high-pitched tones of a modem as he sent or received messages. At odd hours, she'd heard the *clackety-clack* of his fax machine, as if someone rushed out messages no matter what the hour in their time zone. Once she'd heard the noise at five in the morning.

She reached the wall telephone next to the planning center in the kitchen just as it shrilled a third time. "Hello," she said, holding the receiver between her chin and shoulder while she put on a fresh pot of coffee.

The static hum of the line greeted her. "Hello?" she tried again, a bit louder. The line went dead. She hung up, then clicked the coffeemaker on. Sitting on the high kitchen stool, she gazed outside.

No signs of her husband this bright, sunshiny morning.

Overnight the weather had changed. The wind that had been blowing steadily from the northwest for a week now swept toward them from gentler climes due west. It delivered on the promise of spring that March had failed to produce.

Upstairs, Jessica heard the phone in Brody's office ring. It was abruptly cut off on the fourth ring. The answering machine had picked up. A few seconds after that, the wall phone rang again, startling her.

"Hello," she said in a cooler tone than the first time she'd answered. She had a hunch it was the same person who'd just called the office phone and gotten the machine.

"Who is this?" a female voice demanded.

"Who are you trying to reach?"

There was a beat of silence. "Brody."

"He isn't available. May I take a message?" For some reason, Jessica was surprised that a woman had the ranch number. She'd somehow formed the ridiculous notion that Brody had never had a woman there. Furthermore, the knowledge that he surely had stirred up some rather clamoring emotions in her that she would prefer not to explore.

"He is staying at the ranch then?"

"Yes." Jessica wondered where else this person thought he might stay. In town, she answered her own question. He had an office there. Maybe he had an apartment, too. After all, it was a good hour's commute from the ranch to the city.

"And you are?"

Jessica didn't know whether to be amused or exasperated at the blatant probing of the other female. She seemed to think Jessica was intruding or something. Well, there was a way to squelch that suspicion.

"Brody's wife." There, let her think about that.

"What!"

The shriek nearly made Jessica drop the phone. She clutched it firmly. As calm as a cat, she reiterated her position.

"You can't be," the caller declared. "He would never...without telling a soul...yes, he would. Tell him I'm going to kill him when I see him. And I'll see him as soon as the roads are clear."

"I beg your pardon?" Jessica was alarmed. She had a thing or two to say to Brody about women who thought they could drop in whenever they pleased.

"Tell him...never mind." There was another pause. "So, when did the nuptials take place? And where?"

Jessica used her best boarding school tone—cool, snobby and condescending. "Las Vegas. A week—"

The words had hardly left her lips when the woman shrieked again. "That louse. To marry without calling, without letting anyone know...oh, I'll have his ears for this." By now, the amazed disbelief had changed to mirth. The woman was laughing.

Jessica thought Brody's friend was a bit bonkers.

"When did you say you got married?"

"Saturday, a week ago yesterday."

"A week. Oh, I'm going to feed him to the buzzards. I'll never forgive him. What's your name, by the way?"

"Jessica. Jessica Smith." It was the second time she'd said it. Another ten thousand and she might begin to believe it.

"Brody's been on a case in Chicago for the month, and I know he wasn't dating anyone in Denver when he left. Did you meet in Vegas? Are you a showgirl?"

"No. Brody and I met in Chicago," Jessica admitted. Her old school chum had recommended an attorney who knew a private investigator who was very good. She'd met Brody at the law office and hired him over her grandfather's protests.

However, she wasn't going to blurt out the truth about their rushed marriage arrangement, not even to her best friend, much less this nosy stranger.

"Hmm."

Jessica was silent. She could hear another voice in the background. A man's deep tones.

"I've got to go," whatever-her-name-was informed her. "I'll see you soon." It was a promise…or a threat. "Bye."

"Wait. Your name—" But the telephone was dead. Jessica hung up, feeling rather disoriented by the strange conversation.

The oven buzzer went off before she could sort out her feelings. She removed two loaves of cinnamon bread, Brody's favorite, and a cookie sheet of cheese and sausage biscuits that traveled well and were good for a quick snack.

Brody stepped up on the back porch. She recognized the sounds he made—the long stride, then the stomping of snow and mud off his boots before he entered the kitchen. He came inside a second later, stopping by the door to tug his boots off.

"That smells good. I could eat a whole loaf by myself. What are those things?'' He pointed to the cookie sheet as he slung his coat onto a wooden peg.

"Cheese and sausage biscuits. I thought you and Don might like to take some with you to the barn when you miss lunch.''

"Thanks.'' He gave her one of his veiled glances. Sometimes she wanted to ask what dire crime he suspected her of committing when he did that, but she held her tongue.

"Your girlfriend called,'' she said instead.

She busied herself by placing the cinnamon loaves on the cooling rack with a lot more care than need. Her heart jumped nervously around her chest while sh waited for a reaction.

Brody snorted in amusement. "Yeah? Which one?'' He came over to the counter and snatched one of the hot cheese biscuits, tossing it from hand to hand while it cooled.

"She didn't leave her name.'' She took a breath. "I think we'd better talk about...other women.''

He hooked the stool with his toe and dragged it closer. Seated, he broke the biscuit open and took a bite. "This is really good.''

She gave him a tight smile. He always acted totally surprised when her cooking came out all right. "I took a summer course in *cordon-bleu* cooking at an academy one year.''

"Why would a rich girl need to learn to cook?''

"The same reason we learned how to keep house— so we could direct our cooks and maids in the proper method, of course.'' She gave him the most supercilious smile she could muster. It had no effect that she could discern.

He studied her while he chewed and swallowed the

last bite of biscuit and reached for another. "Sorry, didn't mean to ruffle your feathers."

"You needn't apologize." She scooped a spatula under the biscuits, removing them from the cookie sheet to the cooling racks. "Your girlfriend took it hard that you'd married without telling her. Perhaps you'd better explain the situation to her. She plans to come up as soon as the weather clears."

He groaned audibly. "That could only be one person."

She drew a steadying breath. "While our marriage may be a bit...unusual, I won't...I'd prefer..." She laid the oven mitt aside and faced him grimly. "You'll have to tell your girlfriends that you're out of circulation. For a year."

There, she'd said all she had to say on the subject.

Brody's mouth crimped at the corners. The lines bracketing his sensuous lips deepened. He burst into laughter.

She thought of helping his girlfriend kill him. She thought of doing it herself. She hoped he choked on the third biscuit he was eating. She poured two cups of coffee while he contained himself.

He reached out when she came near and caught her under the chin. His thumb brushed over her lower lip seductively, back and forth, softly, gently, as if he were soothing her. When she would have pulled away, insulted by his attitude, he ran his fingers behind her neck and under her hair, holding her fast. He gazed into her eyes as if trying to read her mind.

"Would you rather we made our marriage usual?"

She refused to back down from his sardonic scrutiny. She shrugged. "I'm not as afraid of entanglements as you are."

His expression darkened into a scowl. "Because it's easy to get rid of them if they get in your way? Hire a lawyer and wipe the slate clean. Is that your philosophy on marriage?"

"I don't have a philosophy regarding marriage," she stated. "I've never given it much thought. Until this past month," she added truthfully.

He let her go so abruptly her head snapped back. She hadn't realized she'd been straining against his hold until then. He walked over to the door and picked up a boot.

"Until you came up with a scheme to gain control of your money and buy your freedom at the same time," he said on a hard note. "I once heard that marriage is never free. It always costs, whether to get in it or to get out of it."

She watched while he jerked his insulated boots on over the thick, wool socks. "Has that been your experience?" she asked, curiosity overcoming her sense of self-preservation.

"This is my first experience with wedded bliss." His smile mocked the description.

"Mine, too," she reminded him, comprehending the irony of the situation. Their make-believe marriage was already entangled in more problems than the average for-real one. "I suppose we'll find out the costs during the coming year."

"And during the divorce settlement." He gave her a look she couldn't decipher, but one that somehow contained a challenge. "You forgot to demand a prenuptial agreement."

"It never occurred to me we'd need one," she said slowly, mulling over the implications. She gave him a cheeky glance. "I trust you to keep to the terms of our bargain."

His lips tightened into thin lines. "Don't ever trust anyone. That's the first rule."

His tone was so harsh, she couldn't let his statement pass. "That's a terrible way to live. It would be too horrible never to trust another person. You'd have to forever be on guard because you thought someone was going to cheat you or—"

"Or kill you?" he supplied, bringing her up short as she recalled exactly why she'd thought marriage to him would solve all her problems.

"Money." She sighed. "The root of all evil."

"No." He fastened his boots and reached for his coat. "The *love* of money. That's what the saying actually is." He grabbed an old and battered Stetson from a peg and headed back outside, buttoning his coat as he crossed the wooden planking.

It wasn't until he was gone that she realized he'd never told her that he'd call and tell the prying female not to visit. Jessica clamped her lips firmly together. She was not a jealous wife...

Was she?

No, she wasn't, she decided. But she wasn't going to put up with any philandering, either. Brody could curb his randy male instincts for a year.

Or he could come to her.

Her heart went into overdrive at the thought. She couldn't decide if she would accept him or haughtily tell him to get lost.

If she told Brody to get lost, he'd probably laugh. She hadn't exactly turned a cold shoulder to his caresses. He'd been the one to stop before things went too far.

She should probably be grateful that he kept his distance. Common sense forced her to admit he was right—the fewer entanglements, the easier life would be when the time came for them to go their separate ways.

For some reason, she found that depressing. Maybe she hadn't given much thought to marriage, but she had ideals. She believed it should last for a lifetime.

Pacing restlessly from window to window, she decided she had to work off some energy. The wind had stopped blowing across the narrow valley, and the snow wasn't falling although the clouds still hovered ominously overhead. She would go see what was happening in the barn.

Ten minutes later, dressed in an old ski parka and snow boots, she headed across the path through the crusty snow. At the steep gulley, she found the snow had been packed into a foot bridge of sorts with a bale of straw on either side for supports.

Hmm, it looked as if Brody had expected her to come traipsing over for a visit. Or maybe she was ascribing kinder thoughts to him than he deserved.

She smiled as a surge of something strangely akin to affection for her curmudgeon of a husband filled her. Maybe she would dig through the stone surrounding his heart before the year was up and find out what made him tick.

The barn was warm and surprisingly antiseptic she discovered upon entering. The concrete floor was covered with clean straw in each stall that held a mother and baby. She found Don in one of them with two lambs. He was feeding them from a nipple attached to a bucket.

"Oh, aren't they darling," she murmured. "May I come in?"

He nodded, his shy smile flashing before he concentrated on his chore once more. He held one bucket out to her. Taking it, she felt the pull of the lamb on the nipple as it fed hungrily.

"Where's their mother?"

He shook his head, and his smile turned sad.

"She didn't make it?"

"She was old, that one, but a good mother."

They were silent while the two babies finished their meal. For the next hour, Jessica helped the shepherd with the other orphans until they came to the last stall. "Oh, this one is so tiny. We'd better feed it double."

"That one's for the bone pile," Brody spoke behind her.

She glanced around and knew he'd been watching her for a while. A shiver chased down her spine. Her husband looked ruggedly masculine in a suede cloth shirt with a teal green turtleneck under it. His words finally registered.

"For the...oh. What's wrong with it?" When she leaned over the low fence, the lamb raised its head and bleated at her, the sound so low, she could barely hear it. She scratched around its head. It tried to suck her fingers.

"It's too weak."

"I'll take care of it," she volunteered. She knew she was being sentimental, but she couldn't stand by and let it die without trying to save it. "Tell me what to do."

For a moment, she thought he was going to refuse, then, giving his head a little shake, he showed her how to mix up the powdered nutrient. Instead of putting it in a bucket, he fetched a baby bottle from a supply room and filled it. The nipple had a big hole punched into it.

She took the bottle and slipped into the stall. Lifting the lamb into her arms as if he were a baby, she rubbed its mouth with the nipple. Milk dribbled down its chin. She kept trying, but to no avail.

"It won't swallow," she said.

Brody nearly groaned when Jessica looked at him, her eyes liquid with worry. She held the premature lamb as if it were a human baby, cradled to her breast, while she tried to feed it.

"A lamb doesn't feed on its back. Set it on its feet and hold the bottle where its mother's belly would be."

Instead of taking umbrage at his sardonic tone, she did exactly as instructed. The lamb still didn't get the hang of it. She looked at him again, clearly expecting him to come up with another suggestion.

"Rub his throat."

She stroked under its neck while she rubbed the nipple across its mouth. "Why won't he eat? He sucked at my fingers earlier."

"Wet your fingers with the milk, then see if he will suck."

After letting a stream of milk run down her fingers, she pressed her fingertips against the lamb's mouth, then ran one finger inside his lips. The newborn gave a tentative lick, then sucked weakly at her finger.

Jessica laughed and looked at him, her eyes alight with shared triumph.

It did strange things to Brody's insides. He ignored the sensation. "He probably won't last the day. He's pretty far gone due to dehydration."

"Why didn't you put him on a ewe that lost her

baby?'' she asked softly before going back to making little crooning noises to the lamb.

"None of them would take him."

"Poor baby," she soothed as if the lamb understood every word. "No one wanted a runt. I'll take care of you."

Brody snorted. She'd last about fifteen minutes.

Brody hung up the phone in exasperation. His foster sister, Carly, was determined to visit and meet his wife. Her husband was on a fishing trip with his brother and his son, and she was restless. She was also nearly six months pregnant.

He rubbed his eyes wearily as he padded downstairs to break the news to Jessica. He wondered what his bride would think of having company.

As usual, she was in the kitchen. She seemed to like cooking and taking care of the place. Odd, he'd never have pictured her as domestic from her life in Chicago.

"We have a problem," he announced.

Jessica glanced at him, then concentrated on the concoction in the pot. "Which one is it this time?" The eyebrow with the attitude arched in amusement.

He was forced to admit she was right—their problems seemed to hit several levels. "The caller earlier today was my sister. She's decided to pay us a visit."

"Oh, how nice. I've wondered about your family."

"Not so nice. Where will we put her? She's almost six months pregnant, by the way."

Jessica shook some chili powder into the mixture, stirred and tasted. "Here, see what you think." She held the spoon out to him.

He grabbed it with an impatient frown. She often asked his opinion on her cooking, a first in his experience. His mother had rarely cooked and Aunt Essie had her own ideas in the kitchen. He tasted the chili. "Fine. About Carly—"

"Where does she usually sleep when she comes here?"

"The guest room." He ran a hand through his hair and remembered Jessica's delicate touch stroking through the strands or rubbing his neck... He cursed silently as his thoughts steamed up.

"Well?" She evidently didn't see the problem.

"That's where you are," he snapped. "There are only two bedrooms here, in case you hadn't noticed," he added on a sarcastic note.

"Yes, I have. We'll give her the guest room. I can sleep on the sofa—"

"The hell with that."

One slender eyebrow tilted upward. "I suppose we could share your room. Do you snore?"

"I don't know. What the hell does that matter?" He paced the narrow area between counters. Her scent tantalized him each time he passed her.

"I've heard several friends complain that their husbands' snoring kept them awake. Once I'm asleep, though, I rarely wake until morning. Since you usually go to bed after I do, it shouldn't be a—"

"That is not the problem!" he roared.

"What is?" She stopped stirring and looked directly at him.

"Sharing a bed." Just saying it aloud started things happening in his body that he couldn't control.

She gave him a slow once-over, smiled as if she found his predicament vastly amusing, then went back to stirring. "Ah, yes, I see."

He considered breaking the wooden spoon in half,

but managed to control himself by dint of willpower. She'd drive him crazy before a month was out, much less a year.

"You have a small sofa in your office. I could use it."

"Carly would ferret that fact out on the first day."

"Oh," Jessica murmured. She followed the word with a wicked little laugh. "You don't want her to know our marriage isn't, ah, usual. Is that it?"

He glared at her.

Jessica was enchanted that Brody cared about his sister knowing the circumstances of their union. "I'm surprised it matters to you."

"It doesn't," he denied, a bit too quickly. "I was thinking of you, that you might be embarrassed."

"Why not tell her the truth—that it's a marriage of mutual benefit and will be annulled in a year."

She was seized and spun around.

"There won't be an annulment," he told her. "Not at the rate we're going."

His breath smelled faintly of the brandy he'd had when he came in from the barn. He'd joined her in front of the fire to warm up before he went to his room to shower. He hadn't kissed her again, but she'd thought about it. If he had...if they'd made love there...but of course he hadn't.

"You have too much control to become entangled," she reminded him, keeping a cool tone in spite of his nearness.

He surprised her with a low curse. "No man has that much control when sharing a bed with a woman, especially if—" He broke off as if he'd said too much.

"If she's his wife." She finished the sentence for him. She couldn't help but grin.

"If she's as beautiful and tempting as you are." He corrected her on a harsh note.

She opened her eyes wide. "Compliments, Brody? Be careful, else I'll think you're trying to *lure* me into bed."

"This isn't a joke." He let her go and resumed pacing.

She stopped her teasing. "How long will she be here?"

"A long weekend, she said. This Thursday until Monday."

"Okay. We can surely share a bed four nights without mishap. I'll behave if you will." She tossed him a challenging glance.

"There's no other way. Carly will badger us to death if she suspects anything out of the ordinary."

"So we want to convince her our marriage is…ordinary?"

"Yes."

She nearly laughed at his desperate manner. This was a Brody she didn't know, one who was concerned about another's opinion of their marriage. Why should he care if his sister knew he'd married for money? So what? It was a good deal for both of them. "You want to pour some milk?"

Don supplied her with fresh milk each morning from a cow he'd gentled. She poured the cream off and fed it to the barn cats, thus making nonfat milk for her and Brody. If he was used to whole milk, he didn't say anything.

Distracted, Brody performed the task while she took up bowls of chili for them. She set the food and crackers on two colorful plastic trays she'd found in the pantry. "I thought we would eat at the sofa tonight. There's a special I wanted to catch on TV."

He placed the glasses on the trays. She carried one to the living room. He followed behind her with the other.

When they were settled, she flicked the television on with the remote control. "I'll move my clothes to your room on Wednesday, okay?"

Brody stopped with the spoon halfway to his mouth. "Yes," he agreed after the pause became too long. There was no way around it. He thought of the coming weekend with his irreverent sister and his sassy wife in the same house.

God help him.


Jessica surveyed the room. She'd changed the sheets and hung up fresh towels in the bathroom. All was ready—oops, her book. She picked up the paperback on the night table and tucked it under her arm. After throwing the used sheets into the washer, she turned it on, then went upstairs.

Hesitating beside the king-size bed, she wondered which side Brody slept on. Shrugging, she chose a side and put her book on the wall shelf above it.

She studied the titles in the bookcase over the bed. Spy adventures predominated, but there was a surprising number of bestsellers and mainstream titles, too. The nonfiction works included historicals and first-person accounts of dangerous periods in history. There were none of the historical romances that she loved, though.

Glancing at the alarm clock, she exclaimed and rushed to the kitchen. The cherry pies were ready to come out of the oven.

An hour later, she prowled from window to window. The road held only one set of tire tracks where Brody had left for the Denver airport to pick up his sister.

The trip was his first off the ranch since they'd arrived. It gave her a satisfied feeling to be so independent. With a freezer in the storage room off the kitchen, they could live quite comfortably on their mountain without a trip to town for weeks at a time.

With canned, frozen and dried fruits and vegetables along with bags of rice and beans, plus all the beef they wanted, she could make a variety of dishes. She mentally reviewed her menus for the duration of the sister's stay.

Sitting on the stool so she could see the road, she admitted she was nervous about Carly's impression of her. With a laugh, she realized she felt like a bride meeting the groom's family for the first time. She hoped the sister wasn't as hard to please as Brody was.

Suspicious man. He eyed everything she did or offered to do with a gleam of deep-seated cynicism in his gaze. He hadn't let her help once with the lambs or calves that were appearing quite regularly in the broad pastures.

If the weather continued warming, she was going to explore the place whether he liked it or not.

The whine of the truck engine set her heart to beating like mad. She spied the flash of blue through the trees before the vehicle broke into the clearing near the house. Brody followed the driveway and parked near the decking extending outward from the back porch. A woman peered at the house, spotted Jessica and waved.

Jessica drew a deep breath and rushed to the back door. She held it open while Brody helped his sister down from the truck and onto the porch. While he fetched luggage, Carly rushed eagerly forward.

"So you're Jessica," she cried and gave her a bear hug as if the two women were sisters who hadn't visited in a while.

Jessica wasn't sure what she'd expected, but it wasn't this vivacious female with long black hair and eyes as dark as midnight. As Brody had said, Carly was nearly six months pregnant and showed it.

Brody came in with one medium bag and a small case. He took them to the guest room without a word. Jessica's throat went dry at the thought of the coming night.

"Let me take your coat," she said.

"Thank you. It's wonderful to meet you. I've wondered about the woman who would sweep Brody off his feet and make him eat his words about never marrying. You're as beautiful as I knew you would be."

"I'm hardly beautiful—"

"Oh, yes, you are," Carly declared with a delightful laugh. "How do you like the ranch? Do you mind the isolation? Or have you had time to get used to it? After all, you are still on your honeymoon." She cast a reproachful glance on her brother when he came into the kitchen.

"I love it here," Jessica said, hanging the parka on a hook near the door. "The isolation doesn't bother me at all, but I'm glad the snow is melting. I'm dying to explore. So far Brody hasn't let me outside the house."

Carly burst out laughing at this confession.

Realizing how it had sounded—as if Brody kept her chained to the bed or something—Jessica experienced an onrush of blood to her face. Risking a glance at Brody, she saw he, too, was rather pink in the ears.

"Well, well, well," murmured his sister. She plopped herself on the kitchen stool. "Tell me everything. Start from the moment you met."

Before Jessica could explain, Brody spoke up. "There's little to tell. We met through mutual friends—"

"When?" Carly demanded.

"Last month." Brody gave her a superior smile. "So it wasn't as sudden as you think."

"You had a case in Chicago a month ago."

"I was it," Jessica announced. "Brody was checking into some problems for me regarding my mother's will."

Carly smiled slyly. "I made up all kinds of exciting stories on the way here about you being an heiress in danger and Brody marrying you to protect you...oh-oh, I think I'm on to something by the looks on both your faces."

Brody threw up his hands. "You've figured out most of it."

His sister looked disappointed. "So it isn't a real marriage?"

"Yes—" said Jessica.

"No—" said Brody.

Jessica glared at Brody. He was making her look like a fool. After all, he was the one who hadn't wanted his family to know the truth.

"Well, which is it?" Carly asked.

"We're married," Brody said. "That's real enough." His smile was feral. "But who knows how long it will last?"

"Years and years," Jessica told him. "I don't believe in divorce. Didn't I mention that?"

"No." He headed for the door with a scowl on his

face. "I'll put the truck up, then I have to help Don with the chores."

A blast of cold air hit them with his departure.

"Prickly, isn't he?"

Jessica smiled weakly at Carly's amusement. "He hasn't had much sleep since we arrived..." She realized how that sounded. "The blizzard and...and everything."

"I understand."

Jessica met Carly's eyes. They burst out laughing.

Carly stood and linked her arm in Jessica's. "So, sister, why don't you tell me all about it? The truth this time, if you don't mind."

They talked the rest of the afternoon. By the time Brody came in for the supper Jessica had prepared, they were chatting like long-lost friends.

"Brody," Carly sang out when he entered the house, "you've found yourself a jewel. Jessica is definitely a keeper."

Jessica met his dark gaze and smiled modestly. "Your sister should have been in business with you. She wrung a full confession out of me this afternoon."

"Everything?" he asked warily.

"About why we married." Jessica flashed him a warning with a very direct gaze. She hadn't confessed that they weren't sleeping together. His sister took it for granted that they did.

He relaxed and smiled. "Ah, yes."

Carly frowned. "You will be careful, won't you? Both of you? I hate to think you might be in danger."

"The marriage solved that," Jessica assured her.

"Unless the person kills both of you." Carly looked from one to the other.

Jessica felt a painful constriction in her chest. She

hadn't thought about Brody being hurt. He seemed invincible, but he wasn't. She looked at him with guilt-stricken eyes.

"No one will hurt either of us," he said. He gazed into her eyes. "That's a promise."

## Chapter Five

"The evening went well, didn't it?" Jessica asked when she and Brody were in his...their...room with the door closed.

"You and Carly hit it off" was his noncommittal response.

"She's delightful."

He sat in a chair and yanked off his socks, then went to a bureau and removed a pair of pajamas. They appeared to be new. She wondered if he usually slept nude.

Of course he did.

Sensations poured over her as if she'd suddenly stepped under a waterfall. Ignoring them, she went to the dresser, which Brody had graciously given up for her use, and retrieved her nightgown. She hesitated.

"You may use the bathroom first," he said.

She hurried through her routine and returned to the

bedroom. "Oh," she gasped, stopping dead in the doorway.

Brody had removed his clothing. He pulled up the pj bottoms and tied the drawstring at the waist. "Sorry, I didn't mean to startle you. I received a fax and read it before changing."

"That's okay."

His image burned itself into her brain—the broad chest with its thick triangle of hair, the muscular torso and narrow hips...the manly staff that had started to swell and rise when he saw her standing there gawking at his masculine beauty. Wildfire blazed to life all over her.

She went over and picked up her book. "I think I'll read a while," she mumbled, keeping her eyes carefully on the page.

Brody cursed the entire time he brushed his teeth and prepared for bed. There was no way he was going to sleep with Jessica in the same bed...not with her wearing that silky outfit she slept in.

The lace was cleverly sewn to conceal without totally hiding her lush body. Those high, bouncy breasts were gently cupped in satin with a lace overlay. He could discern the jutting nipple under the blue frothy material.

Or maybe that was his imagination. Who was he kidding, anyway? It didn't matter what she wore or how much of her he could see. He'd want her if she was dressed in flannel from neck to toes.

Entanglements, he reminded himself. He didn't intend to get in over his head nor to lose his head over her. She was just a woman. She'd be gone soon enough.

Taking a calming breath, he entered the bedroom

and nearly forgot his pep talk. Jessica sat with her feet curled under her, her nose in a book. The light picked out the blond highlights in her shiny, light brown hair. The strands shimmered as if painted with gold. He knew how soft each lock was and that it was naturally curly.

"Will the light bother you if I read a bit longer?"

He shook his head. She smiled at him, then went back to reading. He drifted into the adjoining alcove that formed his office and looked over a couple of reports from the agency, but his mind wasn't on them.

He'd stopped in the small town that served the area on his way to Denver that morning and deposited her check. The act had felt like a commitment on his part. Up until that moment, the thought had been in the back of his mind that he could simply hand the money back and walk away. Okay, maybe not that simple, but close.

The situation was becoming more complicated by the second. He rubbed a hand over his face and decided to face the music, or rather, the bed and, he feared, a sleepless night.

He crawled under the covers and switched off the light on his side. A minute crept by, slower than any snail he'd ever seen. He laid an arm over his eyes to block out the light. Another minute. He turned to his left side, away from her.

"I'm keeping you awake," she said. "I'll come to bed."

He suppressed a groan.

The bed moved slightly as she slipped beneath the covers. The room went dark with a *click* of the light pull. He heard her sigh as she settled down to sleep.

After an agonizing period of lying perfectly still, he

quietly raised up and peered at the clock. It had been only twenty minutes since the light went out.

"Do we need to talk?" Jessica asked.

"No."

"This isn't going to work." The light snapped on. "I'll sleep in your office—"

"No, you won't."

"But Brody, you aren't sleeping."

"Neither are you."

She laughed. It sounded a bit shaky. "Well, I've never tried to sleep with a man before."

"Never?" He couldn't believe the implications. He sat up and pushed his pillow between him and the headboard.

"Never." She sighed and sat up, too. "When would I have had the chance? I taught health classes to disadvantaged women while I was in Africa. This past year, I could hardly ask the guard to wait outside while my date and I...uh..."

"I get the picture." He did, in spades. Images leapt into his mental vision—Jessica with her hair spread across a pillow, her eyes closed in ecstasy while he did all the things he'd dreamed of doing to her.

"We are married—"

He threw the covers off. "God spare me from curious virgins," he muttered, removing himself from the temptation that was growing by the second.

She laughed. He glared at her.

"I think it's more than curiosity. You're very attractive in a growly kind of way."

"Yeah," he admitted. "There're sparks between us. Proximity will do that. Sorry, but I'm not going to satisfy your personal need to know what you're missing."

"Afraid?"

"Scared to death." He gave her what he hoped was a cynical smile and beat a retreat before he did the things he'd only dreamed about for weeks.

Grabbing his pillow, he retrieved a blanket from the top shelf of the closet and went into the alcove. He tossed the items on the small sofa and closed the French doors between the rooms. He jerked the blinds down to block the light from the bedroom and shook out the blanket.

It was going to be a long night.

Jessica woke to the sounds of the shower. She wondered what Brody would do if she joined him. A delicious sense of languor seeped into her. She stretched and yawned. Surprisingly she'd slept better last night than she had in months...since the last strange accident had happened to her.

She gazed out at the dawn just beginning to light the sky and gild the mountains. She liked it here. The solitude was peaceful. Solitude? They had a guest. She'd better see about breakfast.

Flinging back the covers, she rolled out of the sack and went into the bathroom. "Is your sister an early riser?" she asked Brody.

He stood with a towel around his middle. A razor was in his hand. His face was half covered in lather. "She used to be."

She waited to see how he went about shaving. He scowled at her in the mirror. She smiled back.

With a little grunt of exasperation, he went on with the chore. She brushed her teeth at the twin sink, fascinated with this bit of male routine. It felt so very intimate to share the bathroom with a man. "My father used to let me watch him shave when I was little."

He acknowledged this information with a grunt.

"Did you watch your father?"

"My father ran out on us when I was five."

"That's a terrible thing to do. My father died when I was six. A three-car pileup. It was odd. One moment he was there, the next he was gone. It must have been that way for you, too."

Sorrow for both of them rushed over her. He washed the remaining dollops of lather off his face and dried off. She moved closer and leaned against the edge of the counter.

"I used to check to see if my dad had missed any patches." She lifted her hand to Brody's face.

He stepped back. "I'm not your father."

"I never thought you were."

They watched each other warily. His eyes contained a warning. She ignored it and laid her fingers along his jaw.

"Smooth."

He hooked the hand towel behind her head and pulled her close. "Don't try any of your sexy games with me. They might work on your society boyfriends, but you're liable to find out more than you want if you try them with me." He let her go. "Don't push me too far. If you do, I can't promise to be gentle with you."

It was a warning more potent than the shaking of a rattlesnake's tail. He stared at her with frustration raging in his eyes, then he turned and walked out, slamming the door behind him.

She dropped her hand, feeling a little sad, a little sorry for herself. Yeah, poor little rich girl, she chided her image in the steamy mirror.

Brody was gone when she returned to the bedroom.

She dressed and made the bed before she left. He had already straightened the office and opened the doors.

She squared her shoulders and went to face him and his sister with a calm air. Composure could demoralize the enemy as well as a mortar shell.

Walking down the stairs, she wondered when she and Brody had declared war.

War it was, Jessica decided after Brody left the house that morning. He'd ordered her and Carly to stay inside.

"Let's take a walk," Carly said as soon as the dishes were done. She peered out the window. "I want to get out."

Jessica did, too. "I have an extra pair of snow boots, if you need them." She pulled a pair out of the hall closet. "I think we're close to the same size." Carly was a couple of inches taller than she was, but otherwise they seemed a match.

"I brought mine, but thanks."

They put on warm clothing and ambled out into the sun. The snow was still deep under the trees, but was mostly melted from the open ground. Water rushed down the gully, forming a small, but noisy creek across the backyard.

"Let's hike up the hill," Carly said as she pointed out the one Jessica had wanted to explore.

"Are you up to it?" Jessica didn't want anything to happen to Brody's sister. That he cared deeply for her was clear to Jessica. It opened a new side to her husband that was very appealing. There was gentleness in him, belying the gruff exterior he showed to the world.

A shiver ran over her as she wondered what it would be like to be loved by this man.

"Sure. I'm pregnant, not disabled."

Letting Carly set the pace, Jessica climbed the rock ridge overlooking the house and home paddocks with her new friend and sister-in-law.

"Oh, the view," she exclaimed, standing on the rocky cliff.

"Magnificent. It's much more awesome than the view from our ranch in California. The mountains are gentler there." Carly cast a sly look at Jessica. "But then, so is my husband."

Jessica didn't know how to respond, so she kept silent.

Carly touched her arm. "No matter why you married, there's something between you and Brody. Don't let him close you out." She laughed softly. "There. I've said my piece. I'll not embarrass you by mentioning it again. But I do think you're going to be good for him."

"Why doesn't he trust anyone?"

"Too many people ran out on him when he was young. He learned never to share his whole self, only bits and pieces. Except with my stepson. He's good with children."

"I see."

"He'd never run out on his child," Carly added.

Jessica didn't think he'd want a child with her. That would be an entanglement of the highest order. She envisioned a little boy with that stubborn look Brody assumed when she pushed too hard into his personal life.

Down in the pasture, she saw Brody come out of the barn on a tractor. Using a forklift attachment, he stacked the bales of straw used as a snow break on a wagon and took them to the barn. Later, he came out without his coat. His shirtsleeves were rolled up. He looked toward the house, then disappeared again. When he drove the tractor and wagon out of the building, the bales had been unloaded.

Carly gave a piercing whistle. Brody stopped the tractor and glanced around. Carly whistled again. She waved both arms over her head to attract his attention.

Jessica knew the exact moment he spotted them. The tension radiated from him as if it were the static hum of electricity from a high-voltage wire. She saw him take in the area where they stood, then his gaze swept the woods and the trail behind them. He waved only after he was sure they were safe.

The hair rose on the back of her neck. She glanced toward the trail, then the woods. It was one thing to put herself in danger. It was another to involve Carly.

Or even Brody. Thinking of him hurt...or dying...did odd, painful things to her.

"Look, there's a deer," Carly said, spying one in the trees behind the outcropping of rock.

Jessica scrutinized the path into the woods. The snow was still too deep to wade through, and she saw no tracks to indicate someone had attempted it. However, the woods were dense and shadowed. A person could hide in them undetected unless he moved. The brightness went out of the day.

"We'd better head back," she said.

"Wait. Here comes Brody. He might like to see the view."

Jessica saw her husband coming up the ridge, his coat slung over one shoulder. His long stride covered the ground at twice the rate she and Carly had climbed. His gaze constantly shifted over the terrain, taking in every rock and crevice.

"Hi," she called when he approached them. "You didn't tell me how beautiful the view was from here."

Anything to distract him from the lecture she was sure he was going to deliver. She didn't want Carly to worry about danger in her condition. She glanced meaningfully at Carly, then back to him. He got the message, but the anger still blazed in his eyes as he checked the woods as she had done.

He relaxed a bit. But not entirely. She figured she was still in for a dressing-down when they were alone.

"You two going to stay up here all day?" he asked. "It's almost lunch, and I'm starving."

"Ah, the way to a man's heart," Carly quipped. "I'll make sandwiches—"

"I'll do it," Jessica insisted. "You must rest."

"I'm not tired at all."

"I'd feel better if you sat," Jessica declared. She laughed when Carly made a wry face. "I've not had any experience with delivering babies."

"Brody has."

Jessica was astounded. She looked at her husband, who was scowling at his sister as if she'd given away the family secrets. "Whose? Why?"

"He's a volunteer fireman for the county," Carly continued when he didn't offer the information. "A couple of years ago there was a forest fire in the area. A man and his wife were trapped at a camping site when the fire burned along the only road out. They had a cell phone, and the husband reported the woman had gone into labor."

Jessica met Brody's gaze. She remembered him saying that females always picked the worst times. Of course that had been in relation to the ewes having their lambs during the blizzard, but the situation with the pregnant woman fit perfectly.

Carly went on with her story. "The husband pan-icked. Brody volunteered to be airlifted in—"

"To go behind the fire line?" Jessica asked. "You could have been trapped."

Brody shrugged. "It was my job."

Just as it was his job to protect her. That's what she paid him for, Jessica reminded herself. The worry in his eyes was for his sister, not *her*. She was his client.

"He delivered the baby, moved the couple and the child to a trench surrounded by rock and covered them with a safety blanket. With the fire coming toward him, he climbed the highest rock and directed the helicopter pilots in dropping water and fire retardant over the area. The governor gave him a medal," Carly concluded with unconcealed pride.

Jessica didn't try to hide the admiration she felt. She reached up and rubbed her hand along his strong jaw. "My hero," she said softly, teasing but meaning it, too.

He scowled at both women. They laughed.

"Let's go," he ordered. He told Jessica to lead the way, put Carly in the middle and followed the two women.

At the house, he left them and returned to the tractor and wagon. Jessica watched him drive across the pas-ture and stop by the covered bales of hay stacked by the fence while she washed her hands at the sink.

"You're in love with him," Carly declared.

Jessica jerked around, startled. "No, I—" She pressed her lips together, not sure what to say.

"Yes, you are." She nodded her head positively. "I can't tell you how relieved I am. Brody needs to be loved. He won't admit it, of course. You'll have to convince him."

"Right, and pigs will fly."

"Seduce him," Carly advised.

Jessica shook her head. "I don't think I can."

"He's fighting it," Carly agreed, "but Aunt Essie used to say there's nothing a smart woman can't do if she sets her mind to it."

"That was the woman who took you and Brody in, wasn't it?"

"Yes. Would you like to know about our life with her?"

Jessica nodded.

Until Brody and Don came in for lunch, Jessica listened while Carly told her about the life of two youngsters that nobody wanted except an old woman who'd taken them in and loved them until the wounds of life had healed.

"But the scars are still there," Jessica murmured.

"And the defenses," Carly added. "To get to Brody, you'll have to get past a wall of doubt and distrust."

"What if I don't?"

"It will be a terrible waste." Hearing a car engine outside, Carly went to the door. "Here are the men. Oh, no, I can't believe it." She tore out the door at a run.

Jessica arrived at the door in time to see Carly enveloped in a bear hug by a tall, blond-haired guy dressed in jeans and a fleece-lined jacket.

"Ty," Carly was saying. "Oh, darling." They kissed deeply, passionately.

"I take it you two know each other." Jessica took Carly's coat to her.

"This is my husband, Ty Macklin. This is Jessica, Brody's wife," Carly introduced them. "What are you doing here?"

"Looking for my missing wife."

"Where's Jonathan?"

"Staying with Shane and Tina and helping with Ian. Their son," he added in an aside to Jessica.

She nodded. "Have you had lunch? We're about to eat."

"I'm starved. That airplane food wouldn't fill a hollow leg, much less a grown man…or a pregnant lady." He looped an arm around his wife and patted her tummy. "Where's Brody?"

"Uh, he should be in any moment." Jessica ushered them into the house and made four more sandwiches. She emptied a bag of chips into a bowl and set it on the table.

When Brody arrived, dinner, as they called the noon meal on the ranch, was ready. Jessica noted Brody greeted his brother-in-law with respect and friendship. She also realized he'd known who had arrived and when. He kept a sharp eye on the house.

He wanted to know where his nephew was and was obviously disappointed that he wasn't with his father.

"He has school," Ty explained.

While Brody washed up, Jessica and Carly poured coffee, iced tea and sodas. The talk was lively and interesting around the table as the three of them caught up on family news. Jessica, seated opposite Brody, smiled happily.

"Brody married Jessica and brought her here to protect her," Carly explained the marriage to her husband when he teased Brody about the sudden nuptials. "Isn't that romantic?"

Her husband looked a question at Brody, who nodded, admitting it was true.

Jessica glanced up to find his dark gaze on her, his expression unreadable. "We have to stick it out a year, then I'll be free of my mother's will. And Brody will be rid of me," she added with a laugh that caught at her throat.

"Maybe he'll decide to keep you," Carly suggested with a hard look at her brother.

"Maybe," he agreed in a lazy drawl that drew a laugh from his brother-in-law.

Jessica's heart skipped a couple of beats.

"I'm thinking of throwing you back," Ty told his wife. "Or chaining you in the house if you ever take off again while I'm gone."

"I called you on the cell phone," she reminded him, not the least daunted by his threat.

Jessica was fascinated by the playful jousting between husband and wife. That they were mad about each other was evident. She thought of Brody loving her that way. The thought produced shock waves of longing in her.

An image of his strong, muscular body as he'd put on his pj bottoms came to her. She wanted to be enfolded in his warmth again, the way he'd held her pinned to the wall in her bedroom that time. Only she wanted to be in bed...with him holding her that way.

A knot of desire pulsed in her throat. She wanted her husband, really wanted him, not out of curiosity, not even because of the flames he set within her. She wanted *him*.

She wanted him to kiss her and make love to her without reservation. She wanted passion and fire with him. All the things she'd read about in books and poems, she wanted.

With him.

## Chapter Six

By the time supper was over, Carly and Ty had brought Brody up-to-date on family doings. Jessica listened with rapt attention as Carly teased her foster brother about hiding his bride away on the ranch.

Much more surprising was the fact that Brody took the ribbing in stride, a tolerant smile on his sensuous lips the whole time, and returned it in kind. "Don might quit if I let her off the ranch. He says her cooking is better than mine," he informed his sister.

"She's much too nice for you to keep her to yourself," Carly insisted with a mischievous grin. "So when are you going to bring her for a visit? Jonathan wants to meet his new aunt."

Jonathan was Ty's son from his first marriage. He and Carly were very close, it appeared.

"When I'm sure it's safe," Brody replied.

That brought a sober element into the evening. Jessica felt the weight of responsibility for introducing danger to others. Until her year was up, she was a menace to whoever associated with her. Especially her husband.

"We shouldn't have married," she said aloud. "I didn't think... I considered only my own freedom. I didn't think about danger to others...to you and perhaps Don."

"That's why I get paid big bucks." His sardonic smile indicated his disregard for danger. Not that he didn't know it existed, but he wasn't afraid of it.

"It must be tough to live with a threat hanging over you all the time," Carly murmured in sympathy.

Jessica mulled the past year over before she spoke. "It isn't, not really. I try to be careful, of course, but I refuse to let it rule my life. And it helps having Brody on my side," she added with a laugh. "He's better than a whole pack of watchdogs."

"Keeps a close eye on you, huh?" Ty inquired with a gleam in his gorgeous blue eyes. "Husbands tend to be a bit like that. We like to know where our women are and what they're up to."

He gave Carly a stern perusal that earned him a quick hug from her.

"Jessica isn't convinced she's in danger," Brody mentioned. "She thinks her close calls were accidents."

"Not really, but there have been only two real incidents."

"Maybe someone is being extremely cautious."

She didn't have any argument to that. "Well, I'm going to write a will and leave everything to charity. That should take care of the problem."

"But what about your mother's will?" Carly asked.

"I talked to my attorney. Now that I've fulfilled the first part of it, even if the marriage doesn't last, I can probably get the rest set aside. If something should happen to me during the year, it wouldn't be my fault, so my will would stand."

"Nothing will happen to you," Brody said abruptly.

He looked so fierce Jessica was momentarily put off balance. She slipped her hand into his and squeezed it in gratitude. He tightened his grasp when she would have pulled away and continued to hold her hand in his.

He rubbed his thumb along her knuckles, apparently unconscious of his actions while he talked to Ty about cattle prices. But she wasn't. She felt the tough calluses in his palm, the rough place where a cut healed on his thumb.

A storm of longing ran through her. Emotions she couldn't identify clamored in her chest. She wanted...she wanted... She didn't know what she wanted.

At last he let her go to replenish their coffee cups. She served the last of the cherry pie she'd made the day before.

At ten, Carly decided to say good-night. She admitted she may have overdone it with the hard climb up the ridge coming on top of the trip. Her husband watched her with a trace of worry in his gaze as she left the family room.

Jessica stood. "I'd better go, too. Breakfast comes early on a ranch, although Brody doesn't wake me when he first gets up," she hastened to add in case he thought she was complaining.

She went upstairs and prepared for bed, her thoughts on the visiting couple. She wondered if Brody would

ever look at her the way Ty looked at Carly, as if his
world revolved around her.

Remembering she hadn't readied the coffeepot and
turned on the automatic timer, she returned to the
kitchen.

"Is it the uncle?" she heard Ty ask in a musing tone.
"He has the most logical motive, but…"

"The obvious isn't always the way of things,"
Brody finished during the pause that followed.

Jessica froze on the bottom step. They were discussing her. She waited to hear Brody's thoughts.

"You've had the uncle thoroughly checked out?"

"Yes."

"And?"

"His investments are sound. Apparently he's recov-
ered from his past losses. That puts a different spin on
the situation."

"Meaning?"

"He has enough money for a comfortable life. Why
risk the fortune you have for one you probably
wouldn't get to collect, especially now that Jessica is
married?"

"Some people become obsessed with money. They
want theirs and anyone else's they can get. It's more
than greed. It becomes the focus of their lives."

"The love of money," Brody muttered. "Like the
love of a woman, it has led to the downfall of many a
man."

"Unless it's the right woman," Ty suggested wryly.
"Then life can be pretty nice. You'll find out when
you get this case solved and have time to think
of…other things."

"Huh," Brody said.

"Any suspicious activity since you and Jessica married and moved to the ranch?"

"There were tracks on an old logging road coming in the back way. The driver got stuck. It was probably a hunter."

Jessica heard movement and realized too late that Brody was heading for the kitchen. She turned to flee up the stairs, but light flooded the area before she could escape. Brody stopped at the counter and narrowed his eyes.

"Can't sleep?" he asked.

"I forgot to put the coffee on and set the timer."

"I'll do it."

She nodded. "Thanks. When did you find the tracks?" she asked, worried about him.

"Yesterday. I check the perimeter of the property every day. Don't worry. If anyone comes this way, I'll know it."

"I'm not worried." She realized she wasn't. Not for herself. "Don't confront anyone you find on the ranch, okay? Call the sheriff and report it."

He tilted his head slightly and studied her. "A deputy sheriff lives a few miles down the road to town. I brought him up-to-date on our problem. He knows to watch out for strangers in these parts."

"Good." She gave him a relieved smile and headed back up to bed. When she looked back, Brody was still watching her. Her nerves tingled at the fierce, protective expression he wore.

She climbed into bed, feeling safe and maybe just a little bit cherished. A ridiculous notion, that. But it made her feel warm all over. She fell asleep at once.

Brody closed the door behind him and gazed toward the bed. His wife slept peacefully, looking like an angel in her blue gown. The lacy robe was laid over a chair. The night-light cast a soft glow over the room. His body stirred hungrily.

After going into the bathroom, he shucked his clothes, pulled on the pajama bottoms and brushed his teeth. Finished he returned to the bedroom. Again he was captured by the innocent picture his wife made while she slept.

In a just world, it would be hard to imagine anyone wanting to hurt her. But the world wasn't just. He'd found that out a long time ago. Jessica was learning that lesson, too. Slowly. She still didn't quite believe someone would harm her.

No one would while there was breath in his body. He'd make sure of it. A fierceness rose in him, urgent and lethal.

He frowned at the reaction. Emotion wasn't good. It clouded a man's mind and interfered with his judgment. He had to stay cool and in control. It was what he was paid for.

Except when he lost his head over his sexy wife.

So okay, he'd be on guard from now on. No more episodes like that one on the sofa.

Instead of making his bed in the office, he calmly appraised the king-size one. There was enough room in it for them to sleep without touching. He was tired. Sleeping with a crimp in his neck and his feet hanging off the end of the sofa wasn't all that comfortable. He could handle a couple of nights in the same bed. Without thinking further on it, he slipped under the covers.

After snapping off the light, he settled down with a sigh. The extra-firm mattress felt good. He planned to be up and out before Jessica woke in the morning.

She'd never know he'd been there. He'd keep his distance...

Brody woke with a satiny strand of hair tickling his chin. Jessica snuggled against him as if they'd been sleeping together for years. "Cold," she mumbled.

He raised his head cautiously and surveyed the bed. The cover was mostly on his side. He must have pulled it away from her during the night. She'd followed it, trying to stay warm.

She shifted again, pressing closer. Her leg slid over his and nestled between his thighs. Her arm crept over his chest.

Sensation hit him, awakening the hunger and filling him with needs he didn't want to acknowledge. His skin suddenly felt too tight to contain his body.

Her leg moved over him restlessly. He smoothed the curls that brushed his chin and tried to figure out what to do.

Getting the hell out of bed was probably the wisest course. Before he could ease away, she stirred again, causing an answering stir in his nether regions. He was hard and pulsing with eagerness to claim her.

Her lips brushed against his chest. She kissed him.

His breath strangled in his throat. She was asleep. She didn't know what she was doing. But he did. He lifted her arm, intent on getting out of bed at once.

"Don't go," she murmured. Her lips nibbled at his chest.

He was close to exploding. "You don't know what you're doing to me—" He stopped when she raised her head and gazed into his eyes. "The devil," he said.

She knew exactly what she was doing. The knowledge was there in her eyes. She watched him without blinking, a challenge in those rain-swept depths. When she smiled, her expression teased, daring him to take what she was offering.

Sweat broke out in a fine sheen all over him. He ought to teach her a lesson that would send her scurrying to the sofa in the future.

With a rough growl, he rolled her onto her back and pressed his greater bulk over her. He took her mouth in a punishing kiss that spoke of the days and nights of frustration she'd caused him. He caught a handful of hair in one hand and dragged the gown off her shoulder with the other.

"Mmm," she crooned when he cupped her breast in his hand, taking possession of the pert globe that had tantalized him for weeks. He left her mouth and tongued the tip of her breast into a rigid pebble.

It took only a second to bare the other side. He circled it with his tongue until she writhed under him, setting off fires he wasn't sure he could control.

"So you want to play games," he taunted, pinning her arms over her head and stretching his full length over her, taking his weight on his elbows.

"No. I want this to be real. Make love to me, Brody."

He sucked a shuddering breath into his lungs and tried to clear the whirling haze of passion from his mind. There were damn good reasons why he shouldn't be doing this. He couldn't think of a one.

"Are you protected?" he finally asked, which wasn't what he meant to say at all. With her hot, silky softness under him, he couldn't think straight.

"I'm not on the pill or anything." She slipped her hand free and stroked across his chest, stirring up a storm inside him with her caresses. "It doesn't matter."

"It doesn't matter that you might get pregnant?" He fought and won a small battle not to kiss her again.

"I think I'd like a child." She smiled.

"What about the kid?" he demanded, sense returning with a stomach-dropping plunge as if they'd tumbled over a cliff. "What happens when you decide you don't want him anymore?"

"Is that what your mother did? She just decided one day she didn't want you and left?"

He scowled at the inquisitive woman who looked at him as if she understood every blow life had dealt him. "She met a man who didn't want a teenage son around. She sent me to live with a relative."

"Your great-aunt. Carly told me of your life with her. She must have been a special person."

Briefly a picture of his years on his aunt's small farm returned to him—morning chores and all the pancakes he could eat every Sunday, movies on Friday night, the first time he'd driven a tractor, prom night and the money to rent a tux like the other boys, burning fall leaves and roasting hot dogs over them, returning from a stint in the air force in time for the funeral.

"I didn't mean to make you sad," Jessica said. She touched the twin frown lines between his brows.

His body still covered hers, but the torrent of desire had ebbed. She thought of trying to revive it, but this wasn't the time. She instinctively knew Brody needed to learn to trust her.

"You didn't," he told her, swinging away and sitting up on the side of the bed.

"We could have our own family," she suggested,

planting the seed in his mind, hoping it would take root as it had in hers. She liked the idea more and more.

He caught her wrist when she would have laid a hand on his arm. "No way. Kids deserve more than being the result of a whim conceived during a passionate moment."

"I agree." She sat up and drew her knees against her chest. "I'd like at least two. That would make a nice family. We could visit—"

A knock cut off the rest of her statement. Carly spoke from outside the door. "Are you two awake?"

Brody strode to the door and opened it. "What's wrong?"

"Nothing." Carly glanced at Jessica, her gaze taking in the tumbled bed where two people had obviously slept. She gave them a brilliant smile. "It's late. I hope you don't mind that I fixed breakfast. I tend to become ill if I don't eat soon after I wake up."

Jessica glanced at the clock. Almost eight. That was late for Brody. He was usually up before six. She lowered her gaze demurely when her husband flicked a frowning glance her way as if it were her fault he'd been detained. She hid a smile.

Brody nodded. "We'll be down in a moment."

Jessica was already up and reaching for her sweat suit by the time he closed the door. They dressed in silence, took turns in the bathroom, then hurried downstairs.

After the meal, the four of them went outside for a tour of the ranch. Jessica and Carly fed the lambs while Don checked over the sheep. Ty saddled up and moved part of the cows and their calves to a different pasture with Brody. They put mineral blocks in the fields for the cattle.

With the coming of night, Jessica found herself more and more jittery. She didn't know what would happen between her and Brody when they retired to their room. She'd always tried to play fair with people, and it bothered her that she was actually thinking of trying to tempt Brody into forgetting his vow against entanglements. She wanted him to make love to her. Beyond that, she didn't let herself think at all.

The two couples played bridge after supper. Jessica and Ty beat the brother and sister team with a final grand slam.

"You're a crafty player," Brody told Jessica. There was a smile in his voice and admiration in his gaze.

"Just good cards."

Carly linked hands with Ty. "Tomorrow Brody and I will beat the socks off you two. Right now, I'm for bed." She patted back a huge yawn.

After they said good-night and went to their room, Jessica prepared the coffeemaker and turned on the timer for the next morning. Brody checked the doors. "I'll be up in a bit," he said when she waited for him.

In bed fifteen minutes later, her fingers trembled as she turned the page in her book. She realized she didn't recall one word of the page she'd just read. Laying the book aside, she waited for Brody to appear. A half hour crept by.

Finally she slipped into her robe and slippers and went to see about him. He was standing in the dark, staring out at the night. She joined him by the window.

"What is it?"

"Nothing," he said. His tone was repressive.

"Aren't you coming to bed?"

He snorted. "Why? I wouldn't sleep."

"You seemed to sleep okay last night…if your snoring was anything to go by. Of course I've not had a lot of experience with such things," she concluded with demure innocence.

"Really rattling the rafters, was I?"

She relaxed at the amusement in his tone. "Mmm, I don't know. I was asleep, too."

He laughed, but the sound was harsh, startling her. "Are you inviting me to your bed?"

Her breath caught. "Our bed," she said, correcting him. "You've been busy all day. Aren't you tired?"

"Not tired enough," he said enigmatically. He touched her chin, lifting her face so he could study it in the pale glow of the moon. "I wonder why I thought I could resist you."

"Why do you have to?" she immediately countered.

"Entanglements. Lives can become entangled in a year and difficult to sort out. I don't intend for that to happen, no matter what happens between us. Do you understand?"

"Yes. You make yourself perfectly clear." She retreated to the bedroom. Its silence echoed the chill in her heart. The coldness was getting closer. She shook her head at her musing. Taking a pillow and blanket, she made her bed in the office.

It was a long time later that Brody came upstairs. She wished he'd come and scoop her into his arms and carry her to their bed and keep her warm all through the night.

Ty was in the kitchen, a cup of coffee in hand when she quietly descended. Brody had been up and gone when she woke that morning.

The television in the adjoining family room was on. The newscaster finished one report, then launched into a description of two burglary convicts who had escaped from a jail in Oregon.

"That's Shane's territory," Ty said. Shane was his brother, the sheriff of the county where the escape took place.

"Do we need to get back?" Carly asked, clipping her hair back as she entered the kitchen from the guest room.

"Maybe. I'll call and see what's happening," he said in answer to his wife's question. "The convicts have headed into the mountains. Shane will need trackers."

He went to call his brother. Carly explained the situation to Brody when he came in.

"Do you want my help?" Brody asked when Ty returned.

"No. We'll have dogs and men who know the area. You'd better continue with your plans."

Jessica cast a quick glance Brody's way, but his expression told her nothing. They ate the breakfast Jessica quickly prepared, then Jessica hugged her new family before they left for Denver and the airport there.

When she and Brody stopped waving and returned inside, she turned to him. "What plans?"

He didn't pretend to misunderstand her. "To catch the person who wants you dead."

"How are you planning to do that?"

"By being here." He gestured at the ranch and the surrounding territory. "He'll have to come to us. The later it gets, the more chances he'll have to take."

"To do me in before the year is up."

"Right."

She sighed and pushed a strand of hair away from her face. "I thought my troubles would be over if I married."

His cynical smile told her she should have known better.

"Life is never simple," she concluded. "You could be killed along with me."

Brody shrugged. "I could be, but I don't plan on it."

She wasn't amused by his confident statement. "I don't want you hurt because of me."

He frowned the way he did when he was thinking things through. "I won't get hurt. Neither will you. I told you I'd take care of you. I will."

With that, he left her and went about the chores that never let up on a ranch. She returned to the house and started on the dishes, her mind awash with worry in spite of his reassurance.

Brody dismounted and left the gelding ground-hitched while he scouted the area. Dropping to his haunches, he studied the ground along the bank. The ford was the only place the creek could be crossed in a vehicle along this entire backstretch of the ranch. The land rose abruptly into mountainous country beyond this point.

Someone had been through here again. The rain Wednesday had washed out the older tracks he'd found last week.

He studied the tire tread, noting a V-shaped cut along one edge that would make it easier to identify the tracks if he found them on other parts of the ranch. He saw where the vehicle had stopped on this side of the creek and turned around.

Remounting, he crossed the fast-flowing stream, high from spring runoff, and checked the other side. No tread there, but someone had stood on the bank and surveyed the area. Then the person had walked up the old logging road to a high point and looked over the land from there.

Brody stood on the same spot, his eyes narrowed behind his sunglasses. Yeah, this was a good spot. From here, he could see Don moving the sheep up the narrow valley to the high pastures where they would stay the summer. The summer cabin was clearly visible from here. An observer could watch the comings and goings of anyone in the two-room cabin, which had only a front door, with impunity.

He used a twig to blot out his own tracks and returned to his horse. Mounting, he laid down a false trail as if a group of horsemen had crossed here and ridden into the woods. He circled around and left the area by another trail.

Riding cross-country, he returned to the ranch house. It took an hour's hard ride. But it would take longer for a vehicle to cover the rutted, rocky logging road from the creek to where the rough track meandered over the ridge above the ranch house.

Stopping on the rimrock, he watched the activity below. The two college students who helped with the cattle in the summer were branding calves and attaching pesticide tags to their ears before moving them to higher ground.

Another figure emerged from the barn. He felt a painful tightening all the way down to his toes. Jessica.

The lamb she'd adopted frolicked behind her, following along as if he were a puppy at her heels. When the lamb grew into a yearling, it would become a pest. Too big to be a pet, it would continue to act like one unless he intervened. He'd separate the two the same as Don separated the ewes from the lambs when it was time.

Time. He could hardly believe three weeks had passed since their marriage. Three weeks of wedded bliss.

Ha.

Jessica had moved back to the guest room as soon as Carly and Ty drove out of the yard. She'd been rather quiet since then. He found himself worrying about her at odd moments while he did the never-ending chores and kept up his surveillance of the ranch. Carly had called to report the escaped men had been captured and all was well with them.

He wished he could say the same for himself and Jessica. It was getting harder to share the house with her. Every night he tossed and turned, haunted by the memory of that one night she'd slept with him.

Shaking his head in disgust at his inability to root the feel of her out of his dreams, he guided the gelding down the steep slope. After setting the horse free in the paddock, he went to the house. Jessica smiled at him from the stove where she stirred something that smelled good.

His pulse leapt as he gazed at her. She was a continual surprise to him. He still couldn't believe the way she'd taken over the cooking and the house. She cared for the orphaned lamb and helped with the chores day after day, her humor intact. It didn't add up. There had to be a catch somewhere, the fatal flaw that would prove it was all an act.

But his doubts didn't stop the rush of eagerness that had him hurrying to remove his boots and get closer to her.

"You went for a long ride," she murmured before tasting the contents of the pot.

"Checking fences."

"What did you find?"

"The usual. What are you cooking?"

"Chicken and dumplings. Do you like them?"

"Yeah. They're one of my favorites."

The only ones he'd eaten was at the diner in town where the dumplings were doughy strips in a thick broth. Jessica's broth was thick, but the dumplings were round. He took the spoon from her and chased one around the pot. When he fished it out and bit into it, he nearly swooned.

"That's the best thing I ever ate," he said without thinking. He was hesitant to offer her compliments. He didn't want to encourage her. She already drove him crazy with her nesting activities. Next thing he knew, she'd be wanting to change the furniture or curtains or something.

"So what kind of tracks did you find?" she asked.

He nearly dropped the spoon. When he looked into her eyes, he realized she'd been testing him. His start of surprise had given him away. "How did you know about those?"

"A calculated guess. Were they similar to the ones you found on the logging road?"

Brody recalled the night he'd caught her eavesdropping on the stairs. "No, but I found a track with a plug gone on the front tire of the vehicle. Someone stopped at the creek turnoff recently. It might have been a couple who parked last night for a little moonlight and romance."

She didn't pick up on his quip about a romantic couple. Instead twin lines appeared between her eyes as she frowned. "Brody, I never meant to put you in danger when I suggested marriage. I didn't think—"

"I charge a fair amount to put myself in danger for my clients." He interrupted her apology. "That's what you pay me to do. It's part of the job, just as it was before the marriage."

"Part of the job," she repeated, thinking it over.

"That's right. This is just a job, nothing more." His heart pounded crazily against his ribs, startling him. It exposed the lie in what he'd just said. Protecting Jessica had been more than a job from the first minute.

"You know," she said slowly, "it occurs to me that I don't have to live with you. I merely have to stay married for the year. My mother's will said nothing about living together."

"It's rather difficult to have a marriage otherwise, isn't it?" he countered.

"I could move somewhere else...where no one knows me. As Mrs. Smith, I'd be incognito, so to speak."

Anger erupted in him. "Any woman using my name and claiming to be my wife will live where I can keep an eye on her. You leave here and you'll find our marriage annulled before you hit the state line."

"But Brody, it would be safer for you—"

"And that's that," he added for good measure, stopping her concerned protests.

She looked into his eyes, her own troubled and guilt-ridden. "I've never been anything but trouble to the people I lo—the people I'm kin to, either by blood or marriage."

He caught the change in wording, but didn't pursue it. "Poor little rich girl," he scoffed.

Her eyes flickered with sadness, but she gave him a

saucy grin. "Rich is the operative word. One year and I won't have to put up with your insults. Is Don coming in for lunch?"

"No. He's moving sheep. He and I will take turns keeping an eye on them until his nephew arrives when school is out."

"I see." She set the table. "If you could do anything you wanted, what would you do?" She gave him an earnest glance before turning off the heat under the dumpling pot and laying the spoon aside. She put the pot on a trivet on the table and indicated he should take his seat.

"Live at the ranch most of the time. I can run the office easily enough from here." He washed up at the sink before sitting in his usual chair.

"How long would you be satisfied to rusticate?"

He turned the question on her. "Are you bored with ranch life? You still have over eleven months to go."

"No, I'm not bored," she was quick to deny. "You seem too active to drive a few cattle and sheep to pasture for the rest of your life."

"It's the life I like."

"Because you don't have to deal with people?"

"Something like that," he agreed.

The truth was, he was restless. He wasn't sure if it was due to having to deal with Jessica living in the same house day after day or to the lack of action. Since waking up with her in his arms, he'd felt the emptiness closing in.

He liked it that way, he reminded himself ruthlessly. Eleven months and she'd be gone. Maybe he should let her go before it was too late. Too late for what? He didn't want to think about that. He ate and left the house as quickly as he could. To linger was foolish.

# Chapter Seven

Jessica listened to the hum of the vacuum cleaner in Brody's bedroom. A totally unwarranted wave of jealousy had overcome her when the woman who cleaned for him finally made it to the ranch.

The housekeeper was maybe all of twenty-two. She had long brown hair, blue eyes with lashes to die for and a sweet smile. She was married to a cowboy who worked over on a big ranch east of them. Thank goodness. Or else Jessica might have felt compelled to fire her on the spot.

Jealousy. It wasn't a pretty emotion.

The first Jessica had known the other woman had arrived was when she'd heard Brody's quiet laughter in the kitchen. Curious, she'd hurried from her room. She'd found him chatting with a young, spritely female who moved familiarly around the kitchen as if she belonged there. Brody had introduced his housekeeper before heading outside again.

He was going to the cabin to deliver supplies to Don. He wasn't sure what time he'd be home, he'd told her earlier that morning when they'd had breakfast. He'd left her without a backward glance and was outside loading an old pickup truck for the drive up the mountain.

Jessica sighed gustily. Her feelings for her stubborn husband were confusing to say the least. One minute she wanted to kiss him until they both melted from the heat; the next, she wanted to pound his hard head with a brick.

After pulling on a jacket, she drifted outside. The wind brought the scent of the pines and firs that grew in profusion along the shanks of the mountains, of the awakening earth that was softening from the melting snow, of the springtime and its promise of life and warmth and all good things. She breathed deeply, hungrily, feeling that promise fill her body.

Longing, harsh and urgent, trilled like a band of bagpipes through her, its rhythms strange and haunting and lonely.

She walked to the rail fence near where he worked. "I'd like to ride along with you. I've never been to the higher pastures."

He scowled at her request.

"Would that be all right?" she persisted in the face of his obdurate silence. He'd been cold and distant since his sister and her husband had left.

"I suppose."

"You're lucky I don't have a brick handy," she said in a perfectly calm manner.

That caught his attention. "What in hell is that supposed to mean?" he demanded.

Jessica clenched her hands on the bed of the pickup. With his housekeeper, he could chat and laugh. With his wife, he could only scowl and curse. "Whatever you want it to," she retorted, giving him back glare for glare.

She turned and watched the llamas as they grazed in the lush new grass of the pasture. One of them stuck his head over the fence and gazed at her from limpid brown eyes, his long lashes fluttering in the breeze. His lips puckered as if inviting her closer for a kiss. Well, the animal was certainly more tempting than her moody husband.

Brody moved so fast she didn't have time to react. His big hands caught her shoulders and whirled her around. "Don't touch me," she ordered haughtily, the restless anger overcoming her better judgment.

*Splat.*

A blob of green spit landed on her white shirt. She stared at it in disbelief. She jerked her gaze upward.

"Don't look at me," her husband said in evident amusement. "I didn't do it. Oh-oh."

*Splat.*

He moved them in time. The second missive landed on the fender of the pickup and slithered down.

Jessica's mouth dropped open. "The llama spit on me?"

The llama gazed at her over the fence railing. He fluttered his eyelashes at her, his expression pleasantly satisfied with his feat.

She could feel the moisture soak right through her bra and on her breast. "Yuck."

Brody shook out his handkerchief. "Sorry, I forgot

to warn you about our friend here.'' He rubbed at the spot.

White-hot heat spread in ever-increasing circles as he cleaned her shirt. Although he held the material taut with one hand, he rubbed against her breast with each stroke of his handkerchief. When she stole a glance at him, there was laughter in his eyes.

''Have you ever had llama stew?'' she asked with vengeance gleaming foremost in her mind.

Brody could contain it no longer. He burst out laughing. His city wife had looked so shocked, then indignant when she'd realized what the llama had done.

''I think I can safely say I've been dissed.'' She gave him a wry grimace and reached for the handkerchief.

''I'll do it,'' he volunteered. ''Mind if I use some spit? It'll take the stain out.''

''Feel free,'' she said in a resigned tone.

He subdued the smile that tickled the corner of his mouth and moistened the handkerchief. Rubbing at the green stain, he felt the amusement fade, to be replaced by feelings far stronger and more tempestuous than laughter.

Her nipple tucked into a tight little bud that brought back the memory of exactly how it had felt when he'd kissed her there and run his tongue over the intriguing tip. His own body contracted, then expanded with a painful surge as desire flooded him. He stopped rubbing and let his hand stay where it was.

She looked at him again, then lifted her hands and laid them on his chest. Her lashes drifted downward. He recognized the signs of arousal in her, the muted excitement as passion began to build. He started rubbing again, around and around the full globe of her breast. He knew he should back off, get the hell out of there, but he stayed.

Jessica arched her back, wanting more. "Brody," she murmured. Her lungs ached as she tried to draw a breath. She moved forward, stretching upward at the same time.

His mouth met hers in a kiss of searing hunger. She opened her mouth and felt him sweep inside, his tongue stroking hers in a fashion so erotic it made her knees weak. She flicked her tongue against his, then joined in the intimate caresses.

When her legs could bear her weight no longer, she leaned against him. Arms as strong as a mountain ash wrapped around her, nearly lifting her off her feet. She was crushed to his powerful frame. His strength shocked her, yet she sensed that the mighty flex of his muscles that so awed her was a bid for control on his part.

Brody fought his own need to hold her even tighter. He took two steps and lifted her to the tailgate of the rusty truck. He pushed his way between her thighs. A roar invaded his head as he felt her heat through the layers of their jeans. Her hips rolled against him, caressing the hard ridge and fueling the fire in him into a roiling inferno.

Without thinking, he leaned over her, pressing her against the bed of the truck, her head pillowed on a five-pound sack of rice. She shifted restlessly beneath him, deep in the sensual abandon of a woman lost in ecstasy. He raised one knee and rested it beside her thigh on the tailgate, letting her take some of his weight. With each movement of her hips, she caressed him.

He pushed closer and heard her give a breathless

moan. She opened her thighs and wrapped her legs around his hips. He moved against her, oblivious to anything but the intense pleasure they shared. She moved from side to side, driving him crazy with the feel of her lush breasts against his chest. With one hand, he freed the fastenings on her shirt, then his. He pushed her bra out of the way.

"Ahh," he groaned when her breasts hit his bare flesh. It was the sweetest torture he'd ever experienced. He dipped his head and caught the taut nipple between his teeth. Holding it gently, he stroked his tongue over it again and again.

She cried out and her hips bucked against him. Heat exploded in every part of his body. When she laid her hands on each side of his face, he let her guide his mouth back to hers while she pressed upward, those unbound breasts like brands against his skin. Her arms encircled his shoulders and whimpering sounds escaped her as he kissed along her neck.

Some wiser part of him, knowing it couldn't wrest control from the wild passion that clamored through his body, issued quiet warnings about consequences and a future he couldn't foresee. He knew he should stop, but he couldn't. God help him, he couldn't give her up...

The sounds of an engine cranking, dying, then cranking again brought him out of the sensual trance. He looked up in time to see the housekeeper drive off in her ten-year-old compact.

She tooted the horn and waved as she hurtled down the driveway at her usual dust-stirring speed. He realized she couldn't see Jessica lying half clothed on the bed of the truck and was grateful for small favors.

After the housekeeper was gone, he lowered his leg

and stepped back. Jessica opened her eyes and gave him a smoldering look that had his heart racing again. He shook his head, denying the need to sink into her hot, silky depths and find the release he so desperately needed.

"I've got work to do," he reminded her harshly.

The hazy translucence disappeared from her eyes. He saw her throat move as she swallowed. She rose to a sitting position and glanced around the quadrangle between the house and outbuildings as if orienting herself in a strange land. She shivered and wrapped her arms across herself.

"Get back to the house," he ordered, gruffer than he meant to be. "The wind has a nip to it. A storm is supposed to come in tonight. I need to get the supplies to Don."

She nodded and slid off the truck. Without looking at him, she adjusted her bra and fastened her shirt, then she walked to the ranch house and went inside without once looking back. Her back was straight and rigid.

He checked the supplies, then threw a few bales of straw into the truck. Straw came in handy for lots of purposes. He at once pictured Jessica lying in a bed of the stuff, her arms outstretched in welcome, inviting him inside...

With a curse, he leapt into the truck and took off.

Jessica put the magazine on modern ranching aside when she heard the truck arrive and went to the window. Brody was back. No, it was Don. Curious, she grabbed a jacket and went outside.

"Hi, where's Brody?" she called, jumping down from the porch and running across the stable yard.

Don's answer was barely audible. "At the high cabin."

She realized he had laryngitis. When he was racked by a rattling cough for several seconds, she worried about his health. "You need to go to the doctor. You might have pneumonia."

The shepherd nodded. "That's why Brody sent me in. He said you were to come to him and bring the lamb. I'll help you load him."

"No, I can manage. You take care of that bug. How do I get to this cabin?"

"Take the county road to the creek, then turn left. You can ford the creek there, then continue up the logging road."

She watched the older man anxiously until he was safely in the sports ute and on his way to the small mountain town twenty miles down the road. Then she opened the gate and whistled for Ram, short for rambunctious.

The lamb bleated and ran toward her at full speed. She dodged the woolly head when he tried to butt her. Hmm, maybe she should tie a rope on him in case he decided to jump out of the truck. She headed for the barn.

*Whump.*

Her legs went out from under her as Ram lived up to his name and butted her in the back of the knees. She sat down in a shallow puddle.

"I should have named you Goat," she muttered, lifting herself from the mud. She wiped her hands on her ruined jeans and grabbed the lamb before he thought of a new trick. She cleaned its tiny feet on her shirt and shoved him in the cab of the truck.

With a beat of excitement, she raced into the house,

threw her soiled clothing into the washer and showered as fast as she could. She put perfume at her wrists and elbows and behind her ears, then, feeling wicked, dabbed it at other strategic spots.

Dressed in floral bikini briefs and a matching bra, she hummed to herself as she prepared to go to her husband. Her hands trembled as she zipped fresh jeans over the briefs, then pulled on a long-sleeve velour top of ruby red. She debated between her gown and sweat suit, then decided she would be practical. And she could use the sweat suit as a change of clothing just in case Ram sneaked up on her again.

Carrying the ham and lima beans she'd prepared for their dinner, she returned to the truck. Ram had chewed up a newspaper and scattered it across the seat. She put the food in the back, folded the newspaper and climbed in. With a turn of the switch, they were off.

She drove carefully along the county road, afraid that she'd miss the turnoff…no, here was the creek and the dirt road was on the other side of the bridge to the left as Don had said.

Feeling lighter with each mile, she made the turn, found the ford and crossed it slowly, her heart pounding as the water formed a muddy wake to each side of the front bumper. Once she cleared that hurdle, her confidence increased as she made her way up the winding track, going higher into the mountains with each hairpin turn.

At last the terrain opened into a narrow valley. The creek meandered through the center of it. Off to one side, set among fresh-leaved aspens, was the cabin. Her heart nearly crashed through her rib cage with its hard beat.

Brody crossed the meadow and opened the truck door when she stopped by the tiny cottage.

"Hi." Her voice was husky, sexy. She cleared it.

"Who's your passenger?" he inquired in his usual sardonic manner with her.

"Just someone I picked up on the road." She jumped down. Ram landed at her heels, then tried to butt Brody before dashing off to taste a patch of wild-flowers near the cabin.

"I brought lunch." She lifted the plastic-covered bowls from the bed of the truck.

Brody took the heaviest container from her and led the way inside. Jessica took in the cabin at a glance. It was composed of two rooms—the living-dining room, which they were in and a bedroom visible through a doorway. There was no door on the frame. There were two cots for sleeping with a table between them. A clock ticked on the table.

"Plates are behind the curtain," he told her. "I'll take care of your pet."

She pressed a hand to her heart. "What…what are you going to do?"

"Put him in with the flock. It's time he learned he's a sheep, not a lapdog." Brody's gaze sharpened when she sighed in relief. "What did you think I was going to do, make mincemeat out of him?"

"I wasn't sure." She gave him a brilliant smile. "I'm glad we're not going to have to fight about it."

His snort clearly said he didn't consider her much of an opponent. Obstinate man.

She followed him outside and watched as Brody tucked the frisky lamb under one arm and carried him to the edge of the flock. She watched in amazement as he squirted glue on the lamb's back and stuck a wad of wool on it. He then put the lamb next to one of the ewes munching on the spring grass and rubbed the ewe with a piece of material.

The lamb bleated and butted against the ewe the way he did when he wanted food. The ewe looked around in surprise. Her nose twitched as she caught a whiff of this rambunctious interloper. She smelled the lamb cautiously, then moved away when he searched around her belly. The lamb followed.

"What did you do?" Jessica asked Brody when he returned to her side.

He smiled. "Rubbed the ewe with your scent and glued a dab of the ewe's wool to the lamb to confuse her."

"Will she take him as her own?"

"Not really, but she'll probably let him stay near. The others will smell her on him and let him stay with the flock."

"Oh." She laughed as Ram tried once more to find the bucket with the teat on the ewe that smelled like Jessica. "What did you use that had my scent on it?"

He hesitated, then confessed. "I used some of your perfume on a handkerchief."

She realized he'd gone into her bathroom to find her perfume without her seeing him. "My best perfume used on a sheep."

He grinned when he saw she didn't really mind.

She took the handkerchief from him. It had dark smudges on it. She recalled his giving her one to use when she'd become teary-eyed at leaving Chicago. He'd kept it all this time. Not that it meant anything...

Stuffing the hankie into her pocket, she couldn't help the smile that insisted on forming. "Smart man," she said.

Brody cut her a glance from the corner of his eye and was relieved to see the laughter gleaming from hers. "Yeah, that's what I thought you would say."

The thing he couldn't say to his sweet wife was what it had done to him every time he caught a whiff of the handkerchief. Nor could he tell her he'd been aware of her lavender scent for weeks and couldn't stop wondering exactly where she spritzed the floral perfume after she took her bath.

He focused on the lamb again. He'd been trying for a week to think of a way to move the lamb into the flock where it could be with its own kind, rather than with humans. It had taken to raising a ruckus whenever Jessica was out of sight. When he'd mentioned the problem to Don, the shepherd had told him he needed something with her scent and explained how to use it so the lamb would stay with one of the ewes.

When Brody had seen her lace bikinis in the laundry basket that morning, a plan had come to mind. However, he hadn't counted on the consequences. With her perfume wafting around him at every turn, he'd been in a state of semiarousal for hours, then to have her come out to the truck and want to trail along with him...

No way. He'd left the ranch in a cloud of dust, anxious to get away before he made a complete fool of himself. He couldn't believe he'd nearly taken her right there on the pickup, in sight of the housekeeper or cowboys...or the person who was trying to get rid of her.

That was really what had brought him to his senses. It had reminded him of the fact he was a hired gun, one year of his time bought and paid for so she could be free.

Anyway, he'd forgotten the blasted lamb. It was only

after he'd realized Don had more than a spring cold that he'd decided to let her come up and bring her pet. He needed her at the cabin so he could keep an eye on her since he would have to stay with the flock. He heaved a desperate sigh. It was going to be another of those long nights.

Her laughter drew him like a moth to light. She was watching her pet annoy every sheep in his vicinity. Ram was feeling frolicsome. Finally another lamb joined him in dodging around the ewes. The two ran like crazy, then gave a leap into the air as if jumping through an invisible hoop. They continued in this vein for several minutes before flopping to the ground, worn-out from their exertion.

He shook his head in exasperation.

"Watch it. You're about to smile," she quipped. "Ready for lunch, I mean, dinner?" Without waiting for a reply, she linked her arm in his and started for the cabin.

Brody sensed her warmth all the way down his side. He could feel changes taking place inside, a softening totally at odds with the hunger that had him hard and aching. There were things a man could get used to in a year: a neat home, good food, a woman in the house...

He pulled free and stepped away from the temptation of her lavender-scented femininity.

Jessica sensed Brody's withdrawal as if a winter wind blew down her collar. She fought a feeling of rejection and lost. Anger followed closely behind.

Leading the way, she sailed into the cabin in a fine temper. She searched behind a curtain along one wall and found shelves with dishes, food and a few pans and skillets. After setting out plates and forks, she uncovered the ham-and-bean dish, plunked a spoon into it and another in the dish of vinegar slaw. She sat in one of the two folding chairs at the card table that served the cabin as a dining suite.

Brody opened the last bowl and found corn bread sticks, crisp and still warm from the oven. "This is a feast," he commented appreciatively.

She didn't respond.

"I don't have any tea, but the mountain water is better than the finest champagne. Would you like a glass?"

"Please." She kept her eyes on her plate while he pumped two glasses of water from an old-fashioned hand pump beside the stainless-steel bowl that served as a sink. When he was seated opposite her, she picked up her fork and began eating.

Her gaze kept drifting to the open doorway of the bedroom and the twin cots that lined the walls. She could move a cot to the living room if she shoved the table and chairs against the wall. At least she'd be in a different room.

But why should she? Brody was her husband. If he didn't like sleeping in the room with her, let *him* move out.

He went outside after the meal and checked the sheep. Two dogs circled the flock with him, both border collies. Ram gamboled along with them. One of the dogs nipped at his heels to keep him with the flock. The lamb cowered, shocked at this unfriendly act, then raced back to the tolerant ewe he'd decided represented safety.

Jessica, watching from a dusty window, smiled and finished washing the dishes. She settled on a stump in the front to watch the sheep and more particularly her husband as he checked the animals over. The sun warmed her through the red velour, making her sleepy. Her thoughts roamed without control.

She liked sharing life at the ranch with Brody. Basically he was easy to please. He never said yea nor nay about her activities around the house, but let her do as she wished. She cooked and cleaned and sometimes rearranged the cabinets to please herself. He and Don ate everything she cooked with a gratifying pleasure in the food and complimented her on her efforts. She realized she was content.

Almost.

There were things to be ironed out between her and her husband if their time together was to run smoothly. She sighed, thinking of when she would have to leave.

The thought depressed her. She didn't want to go. Brody was the one person in all the world that she trusted.

A painful contraction squeezed the air out of her chest. She pressed a hand to her heart and drew in a shaky breath. Of the people she'd loved, only her grandfather and Uncle Jesse were left. She was estranged from both of them, albeit for different reasons.

Her gaze followed Brody's powerful form as he moved among the flock. His life had been harder than hers but similar in that the people he'd loved and trusted had left him, too, his parents for their own selfish reasons, his aunt Essie because of death. Now he didn't let himself trust anyone.

But in a year anything could happen.

She was reminded of a parable about a thief who'd promised the emperor he could teach a horse to sing if he'd let him live another year. When asked why he'd promised such a foolish thing, he'd replied, ''Anything may happen in a year. The horse may die, the emperor may change his mind, I may be pardoned...or the horse may learn to sing.''

At midafternoon, she went inside and rummaged through the shelves for the cookies she'd seen earlier. She prepared lemonade from a mix and took the treat outside.

"Brody," she called, cupping her hands around her mouth. "Snack time."

He lifted his head. For a long moment he stared at her across the narrow green pasture, then he nodded. He finished his inspection of a lamb's hind leg, then came to the cabin. He washed up at a stand outside the cabin and sat on a rock near the stump where she perched.

"I found lemonade mix in the pantry, so I assume you like it," she said, smiling at him.

He didn't return the courtesy. Instead he surveyed the meadow and the woods behind them and the mountains beyond that.

"Have you seen anything suspicious?" she asked.

"No."

"Is something wrong?"

"Not a thing." Brody noticed the way her mouth pruned up at his short answer. He recalled how it had felt pressing kisses all over his chest and making him ache with hunger—

"Why are you so grim?"

He shot her a glance, then went back to studying the terrain. "Why are you so smiley?" he countered.

She finished off a devil's food cookie and brushed the crumbs off her fingers. "Well, the sun is shining. It's the first day of May and spring seems to be truly here, I'm with a handsome man..." She cast him an oblique glance as if to see how he took this blatant compliment.

He snorted derisively.

"Oh, you've been called handsome before and by better women than me, I take it?"

He wolfed down a third cookie and tried not to notice the slender eyebrow with the attitude lofted in challenge.

He couldn't figure his sexy-as-hell wife out at all. She'd gotten mad about something when she'd come out to the truck that morning, but when the llama had spit on her, she'd laughed, then she'd taken his kisses and given them back to him so hot and so hard he'd nearly gone into cardiac arrest before he wrestled half their clothes off so he could feel her skin on his.

Now she was teasing him or some damn thing. He wasn't sure if she was joking or leading up to a tirade. Over what, he hadn't a clue.

Women. A man never knew where he stood with 'em.

Except he had some good ideas. Experience had taught him not to take how they acted or what they said as the gospel truth.

"What's your point?" he asked, too impatient for guessing games and the little innuendoes that women seemed to like.

"My point," she mused. She bit into a second cookie, leaving crumbs at the corners of her mouth. She neatly wiped them away with the tip of her tongue.

He nearly groaned aloud. He wanted to lick them off for her, then stay and taste her for a good long while, then he'd leisurely roam down her neck and throat to those bouncy breasts that were confined in a bra again.

He felt a rebellious need to set them free, as if they were unfairly imprisoned...

Honest to Pete, he couldn't believe the ridiculous notions he was getting just sitting there eating a cookie with her.

"I was jealous this morning," she stated.

He was so startled by this piece of news his jaw unhinged and sagged for a second before he could snap it closed.

"You laughed and chatted with your housekeeper. I heard you from my room. But you're always grim with me, except when the llama spit. But even when you grab me and kiss me—"

"I don't remember any protest from you about the grabbing and kissing part," he reminded her self-righteously.

"Well, I don't object, not exactly, but I'd like to be, oh, I don't know, courted, maybe."

The word almost blew him away. He'd have fallen off the rock if he hadn't had both feet firmly on the ground. What the hell was she talking about, courting?

"*You* were the one who wanted marriage. If anyone is supposed to do any courting, I'd think it would be you." He was already hard just thinking about it, her kissing and stroking him, maybe rubbing his back when he was real tired. "If you want me in your bed, you'll have to be more direct," he advised and drained the cool glass of lemonade, "but it's an entanglement I don't recommend. If you're getting bored, I'll remind you that you were the one who thought you could hold out a year. If you can't..." He let the thought trail off and shrugged.

He set the glass on the washstand and headed for

the fields before he begged for a demonstration of her technique.

She said something behind his back, but he couldn't make it out. It sounded like, "And maybe the horse will learn to sing," but of course, that didn't make any sense.

## Chapter Eight

Jessica watched the awesome display of lightning from the small window set in the west wall of the front room. The one other window in the room was on the opposite side. The bedroom had two similar windows, one in each side wall. For light and cross-ventilation, she assumed.

The cabin wasn't elegant, but it was adequate. Electricity had been added at a later date than the original construction. A single bulb dangled from a wire attached to a ceramic base. The wire ran across the ceiling to a hole drilled in the thick pine wall. Another wire entered the bedroom from a hole drilled through the windowsill. The bedside lamp was plugged into the socket screwed onto the wall.

In the rapidly fading twilight, she could see veils of rain sweeping down the mountainside, but the storm hadn't reached the valley yet. The air was cold now.

"The storm will hit here soon." Brody sat at the table, a book on forensic anthropology in his hands. He closed the tome and stood.

She watched him stretch his powerful frame and raise his arms toward the ceiling. He looked like one of those half-god, half-mortal beings from mythology, as awesome in his power as the storm outside. She wouldn't have been surprised if he'd called lightning bolts from the heavens by a single gesture.

The light flickered. He reached up and clicked off the bulb, then stood behind her, watching the storm.

"There'll be hail tonight," he said.

"Will the sheep be okay?"

"They wear wool jackets."

She glanced over her shoulder in time to catch the flash of his teeth as he smiled. "Ram is smaller than the others." She worried about the runt who thought he was master of all he surveyed, due, no doubt, to her preferential attention.

"The dogs will keep him with the flock, and the ewe will let him huddle against her. Sheep bunch up during a storm. Unless they're spooked by a lightning strike."

"Will they stampede?" she asked, remembering a scene from a Thomas Hardy book in which the hero's flock had run off a cliff and died, thus taking his entire livelihood with them.

"Not likely. There's no place to run. The mountains are too steep for them to go far. That only leaves the valley. It narrows down this way, making it easy to head 'em off."

"I could help." She smiled at the snort of amusement at her offer. She'd expected it. She was coming to know her husband. He took nothing at face value

and trusted no one. Including his wife…most especially his wife.

Light exploded as lightning sizzled as if it were a
magnesium strip. The thunderclap followed immediately, booming right over the cabin. The sound rico-
cheted from peak to peak, drowning out the keening of
the wind and the approaching rain. She flinched as
Brody cursed.

His hands settled on her shoulders. He leaned forward and peered out the window. She squinted her eyes
but couldn't see a thing in the stygian darkness. Another brilliant flash lit up the meadow, limning the
sheep in an eerie glow.

The seconds after the flash died and the crack of
thunder had rolled into a distant rumble, she could still
see the flock, milling and churning the meadow as the
sheep ran first one way, then another.

Brody cursed a streak, then released her. She heard
the click but no light appeared. He muttered another
expletive. A flashlight came on. She saw him pull on
waterproof pants and a slicker over a jacket, then he
was out the door and gone.

She felt her way to the bedroom door and explored
along the wall where Brody had stood. She encountered
another slicker. The pants were way too large and a
hindrance. She forgot about them and pulled the slicker
on. She headed for the pickup.

Inside the cab, she felt behind the seat for the old
parka she'd thrown back there before she'd started out.
She climbed inside and removed the slicker, then bundled up in the parka and rain gear before venturing out
to help Brody.

During the next brilliant flash, she saw him step in
front of a renegade bunch and turn them back into the

mill. Above the storm she heard him call to the dogs, "Jojo, Curly, circle 'em up." She saw him make a wide sweeping circle with his arm while he kept the sheep around him moving in a circle.

To her left she spied another bunch making a break toward the lower end of the valley. She ran as hard as she could and waved her arms like a windmill gone berserk. The lead ewe veered off but eluded her.

One of the border collies came to her aid. He turned the ewe while she managed to shoo the others into the flock. Between the two humans and the dogs, they kept the frightened sheep from stampeding down the valley.

"Let's get them into the draw. It'll protect them from the wind and lightning," Brody shouted at her.

"Right." She had no idea where the draw was, but she followed him and did what he did, keeping the sheep bunched and moving at a slow, steady pace to the west side of the valley.

After a period of time—she had no idea how long; it seemed they'd been battling the elements for ages—she felt the downward slope of the land. The intermittent flashes of lightning showed her the way. Brody's flashlight guided her the rest of the time.

"Okay, circle them up," she heard Brody shout.

The collies went to work circling the flock, keeping them tightly grouped. Jessica stumbled over a rock. She tried to push herself upright, but her foot slipped in the mud. She used one of Brody's favorite curses.

She saw the flashlight swing her way, then Brody's deep voice cautioning her to be careful. He came toward her.

Reaching up to brush a wet tendril of hair from her eyes with the back of her hand, she heard a crack, then saw the flash of lightning. It registered in her brain that the order was backward. The lightning was supposed to come first, then the thunder.

The limned outline of wind-whipped trees and rough terrain imposed by the lightning lingered in her eyes, giving her time to interpret it. When she did, she let out a yelp of fear and anger. A man stood on a high slope above the valley. He had a rifle. It was pointed their way. At Brody.

With a burst of adrenaline, she threw herself up and at him, scrambling in the mud and slick grass, running in what seemed to be slow motion forever before she reached him.

"Brody, a gun," she cried, flinging herself at him and bringing them both down in a tangle of arms and legs.

"Dammit all," he growled. "What the hell are you doing?"

He tried to free himself from her grappling arms, but she held on, shielding him from the gunman while she pulled the flashlight against her abdomen, shutting off its stream of light.

"Turn off the light," she shouted. "There's a man with a gun on the ridge above us."

She felt his quick jerk of surprise, then the light went dark. One arm hooked around her waist and flipped them over so he was on top of her.

"Keep still," she heard him say close to her ear.

She felt him reach between them and do something, then he flipped his slicker off and tossed it behind the rock she'd fallen over. In the next flash of lightning, she could see it lying in a heap. Brody covered her, pulling her slicker in against her sides and hiding it as much as he could. She realized the bright yellow could be seen easily in each flash of light.

"Get the slicker off," Brody ordered.

She did it as quickly as possible. He tossed it on top of his and pushed the pile into a hollow behind the rock.

His hand reached around her neck and pulled her close, his body half shielding her from the pounding rain. "We're going to make a run for the cabin. Between lightning flashes. When the lightning comes, hit the ground and lie still for a couple of seconds. Got that?"

"Yes." Her teeth were starting to chatter. The icy rain slid down the neck of her parka. Tiny balls of hail hit and stuck in her hair.

"Let's go." Brody held her hand, and they ran like marathoners up the side of the draw. "Down."

She hit the ground. He fell on top of her, covering her with his broad body. Lightning sizzled across the sky like droplets off a hot skillet. The thunder followed in a deafening clap. The storm whirled all around them as if they were trapped in the hot cloud instead of on the land.

"Run," Brody said. He yanked her to her feet.

She flew across the meadow with him. The next flash caught them in the open. She couldn't tell if the noise she heard was thunder, gunshots or the wild roar of her blood through her ears. Never had she felt so scared...or so elated.

Brody practically tackled her, bringing them down in a puddle of dank water and churned up earth. He rolled on top of her when she landed with a splash, her back to the damp.

The rain turned completely to hail. It hit all around them and on them, making little pinging sounds like a child hitting the tinny notes of a toy piano.

Jessica felt the balls of ice grow larger, their force painful against her hands, which were holding tight to Brody's back. His head was over hers, blocking the hailstones, protecting her. Wet drops fell from his hair onto her face.

Without thinking, she kissed his lean cheek. Scattered thoughts coalesced into one clear notion—if they were to die, she wanted them to go together.

"This is a strange time to start courting," he told her in a gruff whisper next to her ear.

"Well, I had this irresistible urge," she said, unable to keep the amusement at bay. The whole situation was comical, them wet, lying in a mud puddle, hail pounding them. "The lightning has stopped. Shall we make a run for it?"

"Right."

They were up and away on the next heartbeat. Brody kept her in front of him. She hit the cabin door and opened it with one yank, or else they would have crashed right through.

Brody tumbled in after her and kicked the door closed with one solid lick. He snapped the lock, then dropped a two-by-four beam across two hooks on either side of the frame. She hadn't realized what they were for.

"Get out of those wet clothes," he ordered, turning from his task. Lightning turned the inside of the cabin a luminous green.

"Are you trying to get me naked?" she retorted. Her teeth still had a tendency to chatter, but the elation lingered. Her blood was warm from the run and the excitement.

"You wish," he responded to her jest. "Can you find your way to the bedroom in the dark?"

"Yes. Why don't we try the light?"

"Because I don't want the gunman to know for sure where we are. If there was a gunman."

"There was." She envisioned the images she'd seen. The wind had been wild just then, whipping the trees and bushes into a frenzy. "I think."

She groped her way into the bedroom and found her knapsack. She pulled out her sweat suit, glad that she'd thought of bringing it, and quickly stripped out of her wet clothes. When she attempted to step into her fleecy pants, she had to take a hop on one foot to retain her balance. Her bare rear hit another, one much harder and leaner, one that radiated heat all over her. She stopped dead still.

Brody cursed.

"Don't," she whispered, suddenly wanting him with a longing that was indescribable. She ached in places she didn't know she had. She trembled and went hot, then cold. She dropped the sweat-suit pants and turned blindly.

His chest was bare and just as warm as his backside. She moved instinctively to it. Her breasts hit the solid wall of his flesh. The wiry hairs tickled her nipples, which were already erect from the cold. The contact excited her as his mouth had done in the past.

"Brody," she whispered, loving the sound of his name.

He groaned audibly, then his arms came around her. A rod, thick, hot and probing, touched her, then lay between them like a smooth log as he crushed her against him.

She ran her hands over his muscular back, awed by the perfection of the human body, by the way they fit together, by the wild incandescence in her blood. A sense of unleashed power, like that of the storm, broke over her. She lifted her face toward his.

Somehow, in the total darkness, his mouth found hers.

The kiss was hard, hot, wild, wicked, provocative, pleasing and finally, infinitely wonderful.

She'd never known anything like it in all her days. Or nights. Or hopes. Or dreams.

His hard staff throbbed between them. She shifted a little and touched it. Brody sucked in a harsh breath. She paused. He thrust his hips forward. She took that as an invitation.

Closing her hand around the warm, living flesh, she moved experimentally and heard him catch his breath, then let it out slowly, as if his control was near the snapping point. She'd never touched a man like this, and the experience thrilled her.

This was Brody, her husband. It was his body she touched, this special masculine part that was made-to-order for her femininity. Between them, they could give life to the seed inside her and grow a child.

Brody slid his hands down her spine, then clasped her buttocks. He kneaded the firm, smooth mounds until the flesh was warm, then rubbed up and down. He let his thumbs explore the dip between the mounds and felt her gasp of surprise as he drew a caress over sensitive nerve endings. There were many erotic spots on the body. As if he were a kid in a candy store, he wanted to try them all at once with her.

The only thing that slowed him down was the knowledge that she was a virgin. He didn't know how much petting she'd done with her dates, but he didn't want to shock her.

When she trembled against him, he took a careful

step forward and found his cot. The sleeping bag was already open on it. He clasped her under her hips and across her back and laid her down.

"Hmm," she murmured, "this feels like a warm cloud."

"The best polyester filling money can buy," he assured her, hardly aware of what he was saying. The hot beat of hunger was on him. He knew what he was doing—oh, yes, forever after this night he would never be able to lie to himself and say he was out of his head because of the excitement of the storm. He wouldn't be able to justify it on grounds of the possible danger they had escaped if there had really been a man with a gun.

No, he knew what he was doing. And he was going to do it anyway. He'd fight the devil himself to have her this once. For this night, his beautiful wife would be his.

He kneed her thighs apart and practically dived between them. He stretched his body over hers, taking his weight on one elbow while sliding his hand behind her neck and tangling his fingers in her wet hair. With his free hand, he raked over her shoulder and found her breast.

Perfection. She was perfection everywhere he touched—smooth and sensuous and curvy. Her skin was cool from the icy rain, but she rapidly warmed as he caressed her with his entire body.

It was the beginning of complete possession.

His or hers?

At the moment, it didn't matter. Nothing did but the exquisite feel of her body against his.

She made murmuring sounds close to his ear. His heart stood still, then nearly beat its way out of his chest when he realized she was urging him on with her little keening cries.

Jessica ran her hands over Brody, her eyes closed as if she savored a particularly delicious morsel and wanted to experience its flavor without any distraction. His flesh was warm and very smooth on his back and buttocks.

Feeling brave, she ran a thumb down the newly discovered erotic spot between his rock-hard buns and felt him buck against her. It took her breath away to realize she could affect him this way, to know she had power over him in some small way.

Maybe not so small, she corrected when she felt the throb of his body against her thigh.

A sensation, as if static lightning sizzled all around them, made every nerve in her body jingle with anticipation. She'd never felt so uncertain and yet so sure of what she was doing in her life. This was her husband, and she wanted him.

"Oh, Brody," she whispered, "yes. Yes."

He knew he wasn't going to be content with a quick joining. It wasn't enough, not after all the nights of restless tossing. He wanted the full feast, from appetizer to dessert.

Sipping at her lips was like tasting champagne. The bubbles were going straight to his head. A mist coated his thinking processes, obscuring reason and all the dangers he knew he should consider...but wasn't.

When she moved her hips against him, he nearly lost it and plunged into her sweet womanly depths without thought of her. He held on until he could reassert control. Sweat and heat replaced the damp and chill of the storm.

He slid against her, then eased to one side. He let

his hand drift from her breasts—reluctantly, but there were other treasures to explore—and follow the line of her ribs. He moved down the dip of her tummy and paused where her hipbone pushed against her skin.

Her lips meandered over his neck and throat. He felt her tongue glide along his collarbone, leaving a trail of fire. He took a breath and continued with his own findings.

The thatch of curly hair at the jointure of her legs held his attention for long, passion-hazed minutes. The Venus mound was gently rounded, delineated by the hardness of bone beneath the soft skin. Then he had to move on.

She tensed when he slipped his hand between her legs. He stroked lightly until her hands moved over him again and her legs relaxed. She drew an audible breath.

When he carefully dipped inside, he was elated. She was ready for him, wet and hot and yielding.

Jessica almost screamed with pleasure. What Brody was doing to her was mind-boggling. She was aware of her body in ways she'd never been before. Not only that, but it seemed as if another part of her had taken control, a part that was wild and primitive and very determined to have its way. She could no longer think. Sensation after sensation rolled over her.

Brody's mouth came down on hers, taking her with a force that was new, but not frightening...at least, no more than the totality of what was happening between them. His tongue swept inside and thrust with insistent passion against hers.

She realized he was doing the same thing with his finger, moving gently in and out. A remaining bit of inhibition brought embarrassment at the obvious response of her body to his touch as the lubricant slicked his finger so that he could slide easily into her. She felt a pulling sensation, but no pain.

She turned her face and murmured his name.

"It's natural," he told her, seemingly able to read her mind. "Don't be embarrassed. You don't know what it does to a man to know his woman is ready for him. Besides, turnabout is fair play. I can't hide what my body does when you drive me wild, either."

She felt rather than saw his smile as he kissed along her cheek. His tongue ran a lazy foray over her earlobe and—another sensitive spot, she discovered—down the side of her neck.

So was the underside of her chin. He kissed down to her breasts, then roamed around them, sucking and kissing all over before taking a taut nipple in his mouth. Everywhere he touched stirred the fires that consumed her. She moved restlessly and again felt the throb against her thigh.

Emboldened by his words, she reached down and gathered the hard length in her hand. He didn't move away. She guided him toward the ache within herself that demanded relief and rubbed back and forth, spreading the moisture over the tip of his phallus. He let a breath out in a whoosh and sucked air in as if he were a drowning man. She instinctively knew it was a bid for control on his part.

"You're driving me right toward the brink," he warned in a guttural tone, but he still didn't move away or stop her.

A sense of freedom erupted from deep within. Brody would let her experiment all she wanted. She explored this newfound sense of privilege with greater confidence.

His hips began to roll with her movements although

he returned his attentions to her breasts. She couldn't believe all that was happening between them. Fire and need joined and flowed to the point where they were intimately touching.

He groaned and pulled away from her hand, then slipped further down her body, his mouth running wetly over her, pausing to encircle then dip into her belly button. Another erotic spot.

Finally he continued his journey.

Her breath strangled in her throat when he nuzzled into the curly nest at the apex of her legs. She suddenly knew what he was going to do and was flooded with shock and anticipation.

"Brody," she said.

"Shh," he soothed her. "It's all right. Let me..."

She clamped her teeth into her lower lip to keep from crying out when he found the sensitive nub and ran his tongue over it. She clutched handfuls of the sleeping bag and held on as desire rioted through her. She wasn't sure what she was supposed to do.

"Relax and enjoy it," Brody advised, his tone hoarse and strained. "Relax and let yourself go."

"I can't," she whimpered. "Something is so tight...inside me. I think...I'm going to come apart."

"Yes," he urged, his mouth hot and magic against her.

She surged upward and released the cover. She ran her fingers into his hair and pressed him closer as tension coiled tighter and tighter. She moaned. She cried. She screamed. And finally she discovered it wasn't a matter of letting go. It was a matter of shattering. She did. Loudly. Urgently.

Brody thought he was going to come apart with her as she writhed under him. He held her hips in his hands and helped her move in a smoother rhythm so that the climax would be complete. Her little exclamations of "oh, oh, oh," were almost continuous now and her movements were less frantic. Finally she sighed and slumped down on the cot, her energy spent.

He raised himself over her and nudged her legs further apart. He had no protection, nothing to defend himself against deeper involvement and the entanglements he dreaded, but at the moment none of that mattered. Maybe tomorrow the regrets would come, or if there was a child, but for now…

She was still hot and moist and now, very relaxed. He held himself in position and started the journey inside. She moved a little. He paused, then realized she was trying to accommodate his entry.

He pushed harder. He couldn't detect the intact membrane—his body felt only its own hot, wild pleasure at this moment—but he knew it was there. He would hurt her, but he couldn't stop. Lord help him, he couldn't turn back now, not unless she said no.

She didn't.

Making soft sounds of encouragement, she began to rub his arms and shoulders. She caressed his neck, then slid down his chest and along his sides to his hips. To his surprise, she tugged at him, wanting him to move faster.

Taking a breath, he pushed forward. She sighed, then stretched her legs farther apart and rubbed one foot against the side of his calf as she bent her knee and drew her leg up. It gave him better access to those sweet depths.

By dint of will, he kept from plunging in like a stallion on a rampage and made the journey very slowly, very carefully. At last the trip was made. He was as far into her as he could get. Pressing, he felt the delicate feminine mound against the apex of his legs. Their bodies were meshed completely.

"I wasn't positive it would fit," she murmured with a shaky laugh when he rested, his head beside hers on the pillow, his breath coming in shallow draughts.

He felt he'd run a mile straight uphill. His control was as shaky as her laughter. "I knew it would be like this."

"How?"

"Heaven." He flexed and withdrew, then began the mind-blowing descent all over again. He felt her hold her breath, then exhale when he rested again. Her hips moved a fraction.

Pride made him want to shout in delight. He'd pleasured his woman so much her first time that she wanted him again. He didn't think she was aware of it yet. She was still coming down mentally, but her body was starting to soar again.

He covered her face with kisses before taking her mouth and letting her feel his hunger through the thrusting of his tongue. He could taste the sweet dew of her passion and knew she would, too, when her tongue slid over his.

She explored this new knowledge tentatively. He held still and let her dip into his mouth, knowing her experience with all the facets of making love increased with each moment.

"You taste of me," she finally said.

"Someday you'll do that for me," he told her, planting the seeds of more exploration between them for the future. He knew they could never go back to their chaste life. Not now. The passion was too explosive for either of them to withdraw.

He moved his hand between them and rubbed steadily until she began her little moans and cries all over. When he knew he wasn't going to hold on another second, she went perfectly still, then tumbled over the edge. He paused, then thrust heavily, his control gone, as the most powerful climax of his life rolled over him like a wild storm tide. He threw back his head and emitted a guttural cry of release and triumph, as primal as life itself.

## Chapter Nine

*What does one say to a naked man?*

Jessica circled the pads of her fingers on Brody's skin at his side and thought of what she'd like to say. An expression of gratitude didn't seem adequate for all that she'd experienced.

Since he seemed to have felt everything she did, maybe no comment was necessary. "The afterglow is just like in books I've read," she murmured. "Like floating. Like dreaming, only you know you're awake."

"Are you going to sleep?" he asked in a throaty murmur. He moved off her, severing the contact, and lay beside her.

She turned toward him, her forehead against his chest. "Not yet. Are you?"

"No." His lips caressed her temple.

There were other words she didn't dare say or even

admit to herself. He'd warned her about entanglements often enough. She held those words inside, afraid to acknowledge them. But she knew what they were.

She felt him move. He groped on the floor and came up with his shorts. "Open," he said, nudging her thigh.

Startled, she obeyed and felt him tuck the cotton between her legs. Warm fuzzies flowed over her at his care. "You're wonderful," she told him, hearing the contentment in her voice. "Everything was wonderful."

"Everything?"

"Yes." The burning sensation had been a fleeting thing, then she'd been aware of a fullness that was new and different but not terribly uncomfortable. When he'd stroked her again, she'd nearly fainted. The climax had been even more powerful than the first time. "I had no idea..."

"None?" He lifted himself to an elbow and began touching her breasts.

She heard the laughter in his voice. Brody, the taciturn, the grim, was being playful. "Not in my wildest dreams."

He kissed the side of her mouth and tickled the corner with his tongue. "So now you know."

"Yes. Show me again." She lifted her face so he could fully reach her lips. He accepted the invitation.

If someone had held a gun to her head and demanded she explain the difference between this kiss and all the others they'd shared up to this point, she wouldn't have been able to.

It was different, she would have said.

That was the sum of her conscious knowledge. The rest was a deep, primitive feeling that blended with the hunger and need he induced in her, plus the vague longing she'd had for other things in her life. With Brody, she'd found them.

The cabin was cold, but on that narrow cot, wrapped in Brody's arms, she didn't need the sleeping bag to keep her warm. With him holding her, she was warm all the way to the center of her heart.

As his kisses became deeper, the warmth became heat, and the heat became a fire that consumed her every thought. The world collapsed to this place, this time and the joining of their bodies into the wild cadence of passion once again.

The storm passed. The clouds parted and disclosed the bright face of the moon. She didn't heed any of that. Her world was here, with this man.

Brody couldn't have faced down a tame cat at that moment. He'd never experienced anything so deep, so draining. He knew he should move, that his weight was too much for her slender build, but he couldn't. Right where he was, that was where he wanted to stay. He pressed his face into the pillow and breathed deeply as his body's need for oxygen caught up with the demands he'd placed on it during the past minutes. The scent of lavender filled his senses, making him dizzy again.

When he finally lifted his head and rolled to the side of her, he saw the flash of her smile in the pale play of moonlight across their bed. He wanted to step into that smile and stay there the same as he wanted to stay inside her even though his body was spent. She touched something inside him—this woman who was worlds above him in wealth and breeding—that made him want to linger and bask in her good will. He wanted her cries of ecstasy, her smiles of joy...

He frowned. Such thoughts were folly. He had to

stay in control. A simple reminder that he'd been bought and paid for, as a bodyguard, not a husband, did the trick. And he sure as hell wasn't going to be a plaything for any woman, especially his very rich, very passionate wife.

However, he also knew that passion, like a magic genie once unleashed, was hard to get back in the bottle. Maybe impossible.

"You'd better get on your cot," he said. "There's a clean sleeping bag—"

Her arms tightened around him. "You're not kicking me out in the cold now that you've had your way with me, so forget it," she told him in no uncertain terms. But there was laughter in her voice. He could hear it as if it were the tinkling of fairy bells far away, enticing mortals to join them.

He struggled between what he should do—get the hell out of the bed—and what he wanted to do—stay with her and make love all night. When she threw a leg over his, rested her arm over his middle and snuggled her nose into the groove of his neck, he lost the battle.

Grimly he pulled the cover over them and settled beside her on the narrow cot. He wouldn't sleep a wink the whole night...no way...not with her breast poking his side and that curly patch of hair against his thigh, reminding him of the pleasure to be shared...he should get up...but the cot was comfortable...he should sleep on the other one...but this one was warm...so very warm....

Jessica woke when Brody stirred. She opened her eyes and gazed into his. His expression was guarded. She hesitated, then, unable to stop herself, she squeezed him and planted several kisses on his darkly furred chest. The curly hairs tickled her nose. She laughed and chased the tickle away by rubbing her nose on him.

"If you'll let me up, I'll stoke the stove and start the coffee," he said in a sleep-roughened voice. He cleared his throat a couple of times.

"Um, I might keep you here all day," she playfully retorted and nipped at the prickly hairs with her lips.

He tensed all the way down his length, then in spite of his distant attitude, she felt his body begin to rise and harden.

"Well, at least one part of you can't resist me." She raised on one elbow and gave a definitely triumphant smile.

"Don't let it go to your head," he suggested in a repressive manner. "That happens to a man when he's in bed with a woman. Any man. Any woman," he added for good measure.

Nothing he said could suppress the sense of well-being and confidence she felt. "But never to me."

She stretched luxuriously, careful not to fall off the cot. She'd never slept this close to another human that she could recall. She felt wonderfully rested, albeit a tiny bit stiff.

New exercise, new muscles, she recalled her PE teacher's advice if the girls complained of being sore when the basketball season started each year. She laughed softly. New muscles indeed. She caressed his growing tumescence.

He swung out of bed. She ogled his masculine form as he pulled on the cold, damp jeans he'd worn the previous day, then giggled at his grimace and the chill-bumps that raced up his body. "The bed is warm," she suggested seductively.

Before tending to the fire in the wood-burning stove, he surveyed the outside from all the windows. Seemingly satisfied that all was well, he shook out the ash box under the stove, added kindling inside, squirted it with kerosene and struck a big wooden match on the top of the stove.

The kerosene caught with a *whoosh*, igniting the kindling. He added bigger pieces of wood. In a few minutes, the fire was crackling brightly. He turned on a burner of a two-position electric hot plate and put on a pot of coffee. In a minute, it added its merry perking to the ambience.

While the cabin was warming, he pumped a basin of water and, to her surprise, hung a blanket between the rooms before washing up. Brody, shy? When he quit splashing and took the blanket down, he padded into the bedroom, opened a trunk in the corner and pulled out clean clothes.

Her breath became tangled in her throat, and for a second she couldn't get it to go in or out. He was arrogantly, flagrantly and so very handsomely nude.

He dressed quickly, then took their damp clothing and hung the pieces on hooks near the stove.

Jessica plumped the pillow up and lay with her hands under her head, watching through the doorway as Brody did the domestic chores. He searched in the pantry and came up with corned beef hash, eggs and bread.

"Are you going to stay in bed grinning all day?" he asked when she made no move to get up.

She batted her lashes at him, exulting in a sense of certainty and...and *power* she'd never before experienced.

Her past dealings with people were influenced by the deaths of her grandmother and parents, the reserve of her grandfather and the uncertainty concerning her uncle's intentions toward her, all combining to make her wary of others.

There had followed her years in boarding school and college, where she'd been just another quiet, hard-working student. It wasn't until she met Brody that she'd begun to feel secure with another person. Before last night, she'd never had this sense of intimacy with anyone.

"Breakfast in bed would be nice. It's warm here." She gave him a deliberately sultry glance.

He snorted a "huh" and continued to prepare the meal.

She heard some banging around, then he returned to the bedroom. He placed the stainless-steel basin on the trunk along with a sliver of soap, a towel and a wash-cloth.

"You'd better use it while it's hot," he suggested and retreated to the other room. He put the blanket back in place.

Jessica was amazed at his consideration. She jumped out of bed, winced, then moved a bit slower. She washed in the warm water, dug her toothbrush from the knapsack, used it and put on her sweat suit and a clean pair of socks. After running a brush through her tangled curls, she carried the basin into the other room. "What do I do with this?"

"Pour it down the drain."

She looked around in confusion.

He took it from her, opened the front door and tossed the water outside.

Putting her hands on her hips, she studied him. "Yes," she concluded, "there is a gleam in those dark, mysterious eyes. Mr. Smith is pleased with his little joke on his city slicker wife.''

*Wife.* Saying the word out loud sent a tingle through every nerve in her body. She was well and truly that.

He cast her an oblique glance, but went on stirring the corned beef hash. Her stomach growled impatiently. She realized she was starved.

''I suppose the bathroom facilities are also outside?''

He dumped the browned hash on a plate, then cracked four eggs into the skillet. ''Around back.''

She sighed and put on her shoes. The sneakers and the parka were still damp, but she bravely faced the chill morning air and found the outhouse as promised, set back in the trees a hundred feet behind the cabin.

''A day of firsts,'' she mentioned when she returned. ''My first trip to an outhouse—which is quite different from those portable toilets at the national parks, I might add—and my first morning to wake in bed with a man.''

He gave another snort and took up the eggs. The bread was toasting on the woodstove. He forked two slices on one plate and four on another.

She joined him at the card table. He split the eggs and hash between them. She pushed one egg and half the hash back on his plate. He set two mugs of coffee and a jar of jelly on the table. Breakfast was ready. She took her seat. He took his.

''Wait. My mother always said you should start the day off with a kiss.''

The black slashes that were his eyebrows jerked upward in surprise, then down in a warning scowl. She smiled, not quite so confident as she'd been upon waking. He didn't seem to feel the same sense of connection that she felt.

"Or we could just shake hands," she added brightly. She picked up the coffee cup and noticed a tremor in her fingers.

"And come out fighting?" he asked with a cynical twist.

She frowned, perplexed at his question, then realized that her words combined with his were those of a referee before a boxing match. "I didn't know we were at war."

Brody noticed the diminishing perkiness in Jessica's behavior and felt guilt spread over his conscience as if it were a rash.

Damn. He had known life was going to get complicated with her around. After last night, it was going to be one giant serving of trouble. He shouldn't have... It was too late for regret. The deed was done.

Sucking in a deep breath, he leaned across the table, hooked a hand behind her neck and gave her a kiss that curled his toes. He let her go, picked up his fork and gave her an inquiring glance. "Now can we eat?" he asked in mock-patient tones.

She nodded her head. When she set her cup down, she was smiling again. He was relieved.

That worried him, too.

God, he'd drive himself crazy if he predicated everything he did upon her feelings and moods first. His job was to protect her. He needed a clear head for that. That was what he had to remember when hormones threatened to overcome sense.

As had happened last night.

"Jessica, about last night." He waited until she looked up. The wariness was back in her eyes. He hesitated, swallowed, then tried again. "It was the best I've ever known."

He couldn't believe he'd said that. He'd meant to caution her about their circumstances and keeping their heads and all that. Last night had been a...a... He couldn't bring himself to call it a mistake. It was the most powerful sensation he'd ever experienced.

"Thank you, Brody. It was that way for me, too."

He made his smile droll. "Well, considering it was your first experience, that goes without saying."

She laughed again, that magical sound that made him think of fairy dells and such nonsense. He sighed. Last night was definitely going to make his job that much harder.

His job wasn't all that was hard. He shifted uncomfortably on the chair. Between cold logic and a hot libido, he waged a silent tug-of-war to keep from stripping his sexy, passionate wife and taking her back to bed for an hour or so.

He stuffed his mouth full of eggs and corned beef before he lost another battle of the bulge...so to speak. He groaned at the stupid pun and ate faster. He needed to get outside. There was work to be done.

"What do we do today?" she asked as if reading his mind. She counted the chores. "Check on the sheep, of course. I wonder how poor Ram made it through the night. Then we need to call and find out how Don is feeling and see how the new hands fared during the storm. What's after that?"

"I'm going to have a look on the ridge. I'll see if I can spot any tracks."

"Good idea. I'm not certain what I saw. I mean, with the wind whipping the trees and bushes around and it being so dark, maybe I saw something that wasn't there, like taking one of those inkblot tests. Different people see different things, don't they?"

"Yeah."

With their chores set out for the day, Jessica ate quickly and finished the same time as Brody. She felt her jeans drying by the stove and found them damp but not terribly so. She washed the dishes while he checked his clothes and banked the embers in the stove.

When they were ready to leave, he told her, "I want you to stay here today, Keep the door locked and don't let anyone in."

"No. I'm going with you."

"Jessica—"

"And that's that," she added, throwing words he'd used to her in his face.

"It's too dangerous. You get me...distracted."

Her smoky gray eyes roamed down his body. She crossed her arms over her chest and gave him glare for glare.

Heat shifted into his groin. "Hell," he said, not feeling up to an argument. "Get your coat and let's go."

She nodded and was gracious enough not to gloat. She grabbed the old parka off its hook and was ready in a split second. Without having to fix her hair and makeup and all the other things a woman did before she left the house. The fastest female he'd ever met. He shook his head in wonder.

Yeah, his rich, city slicker wife surprised him in more ways than one. The trouble was, he was beginning to like them all.

Jessica fended off Ram who was joyously trying to leap all over her. She held the bucket to him and let him suck the milk supplement until his tummy stuck out to each side. "Glutton," she murmured, scratching his ears.

She looked up to find Brody watching them with an intensity that warmed and thrilled her. She wished she could tell what he was thinking. Not tender thoughts of love, she concluded when he frowned and went back to his task.

He was studying the ground near their slickers. The spot where they'd lain in the mud with the hail pelting them, his body over hers, protective and provocative.

She sighed, thinking of the night spent in his arms. When Ram finished, she shooed him off, rinsed the bucket and put it in the shed next to the cabin.

"Ready?" Brody asked.

She nodded. They climbed in the truck and headed down the valley. He stopped before they crossed the creek and turned onto the paved road. She was shocked when he removed a handgun from the glove box and tucked it in his pants, his shirt hiding the weapon from view. She followed him up the hill.

"Stay behind me and do what I tell you," he ordered.

"All right."

He cast her a skeptical glance, as if he doubted he could depend on her. She'd show him.

She followed him up the slope without saying a word. She scanned the ground when he did. All she saw were runnels from the heavy rains. Any tracks would have been washed out.

At the top of the hill, she exclaimed aloud. She had an absolutely clear view of the cabin and the valley. She could see the sheep and the two collies guarding them. She even picked out Ram and his playmate annoying the patient old ewe who let him stay close. Then she watched Brody.

He searched the ground as if he were a squirrel looking for a nut he'd buried in the vicinity but couldn't remember exactly where. Finally he gave a little grunt of satisfaction and picked up an object. She moved closer.

"What is it?"

"A spent casing."

She stared at the remains. "Someone was shooting at us. I'd hoped I'd imagined it."

"He wasn't trying to kill us," Brody told her. "He was firing rock salt."

That information meant nothing to her.

"He was trying to stampede the sheep by shooting pellets of salt at them."

"Why?"

"That's a good question," he muttered, his gaze roaming over the valley while he thought. "Whoever it was didn't want his shots to be detected."

"So it wouldn't look like murder?" she asked, realizing all the grim possibilities. She'd almost convinced herself that her trustees and grandfather had been paranoid about her getting killed. Being with Brody at the ranch had induced a false sense of security.

"Yeah." He laughed cynically. "Maybe the hired gun thought the lightning would get us or the sheep would trample us to death in a stampede."

"What hired gun?"

Brody gave her one of his calculating perusals before answering. "You don't think whoever wants you out of the way is going to do the dirty work himself, do you?"

She shook her head solemnly.

Her husband looked around a bit more. "There's nothing here. Let's go home."

At the paved road, Brody cursed and braked to a jarring halt. He was out of the truck in a flash. Jessica, her heart in her throat, watched as he bent over some clearly defined tracks of mud where another vehicle had left the same dirt road and headed for town. The tracks disappeared in a short distance, otherwise they could have followed the culprit to his door.

Brody returned, his expression grim. A chill touched her neck. She laid her hand on his thigh, needing his warmth to ward off the cold that threatened her heart. After a second, he put his hand over hers, his broad palm covering hers completely. She realized he did it to comfort her.

He headed for Don's house as soon as he pulled into the ranch yard and killed the engine. Jessica jumped down and followed. "I want to see how Don feels," she stated defensively when her husband frowned at her.

Don was better. He had three bottles of pills to ensure it, he told them. He'd also made a big pot of mutton chunks and vegetables to keep his strength up. One of the students had brought him a batch of cookies from the bakery in town.

"Send them up to keep an eye on the sheep when they come back to the house. There won't be any trouble, but I want someone up there tonight."

After she and Brody were on their way to town, she asked, "How do you know there won't be trouble tonight?"

"The guy knows what he's doing."

"A professional." The thought was depressing. Someone hated her enough to send a hired gun after her.

"A skilled amateur," he said, correcting her.

"I'm nothing but trouble to everyone."

"Don't start feeling sorry for yourself."

Anger rose like bile in her throat. "I want to know who it is. I want this to end. I want a life," she concluded on a quieter, sadder note.

"Poor little rich girl." But there was understanding in the glance he flicked her way before turning his attention to the traffic on the busy main street of the town.

Jessica trailed after Brody to the bank. She realized she had very little money in her purse. Not that she'd used any since she'd arrived, but there were some personal items that she needed before they returned to the ranch.

"I'd better open an account," she told Brody. "I'll need funds if I'm to stay here for a year."

"It isn't necessary. You're my wife."

To her amazement, he escorted her to the teller window, told the woman who she was and that was that. The friendly teller let her cash a check without a qualm. "It's a pleasure to meet the woman who finally roped this maverick in," she said, then laughed at Brody's scowl. "Don't give him any slack," she advised.

"She'd better not give me any sass."

Jessica huffed indignantly. She'd been as good as gold that morning, following his instructions to the tee.

He cast her an oblique look, then ruffled her hair and laughed. Her heart puddled in her toes. He was so incredibly handsome when he smiled.

"I'm going to dedicate my life to giving him a hard time," she confided to the teller. "How do I arrange to move my accounts here?"

"Fill out this form and take it to the manager. She's in her office now. Just go on in when you're ready."

The teller handed her a form and pointed out the young woman in a corner office.

Brody walked across the room with her when she finished the form, but stopped outside the office. Jessica took his hand and pulled him inside. She had no secrets from him. None at all.

A smile tickled the corners of her mouth. Brody knew her as no other human did. Passion was a very intimate act.

The newly discovered jealousy rose as she thought of other women who knew his body as well as she did, perhaps better.

"Good morning," the manager greeted them. "Mr. Smith, isn't it?" She looked a question at Jessica.

"This is my wife, Jessica. She wants to open an account."

"Of course. Please be seated. Would you like some coffee or tea?" She was Miss Cordiality.

Jessica wondered if she would have gotten the same treatment if she'd been alone. She realized the jealousy was showing again. She might have bought his services, but she didn't own Brody. No woman ever would.

When they left the bank, he asked, "Do you think you'll be here long enough to spend that amount?"

She stopped. "What do you mean?"

"I'm pretty sure we'll have your case solved before long. You'll be free to do whatever you want. You'll have the freedom you said you wanted."

"How? Did you see something? Who—" She stopped abruptly, not sure she wanted to know.

"I don't know who...yet."

That ominous pause told Jessica he had a good

hunch, though. The cold formed an icy patch on her heart. Her uncle must need money again.

"Hey, Nick," Brody called suddenly. "Wait up."

A man dressed in the uniform of a deputy sheriff turned toward them. He waited until they caught up with him. He and Brody shook hands, then hit each other on the shoulder the way men do when they're glad to see each other.

When Brody introduced her as his wife, the deputy didn't hide his surprise. "Congratulations, Smith, you got yourself a beauty."

"Yeah, the pick of the litter," Brody agreed.

Jessica hit him in the ribs with her elbow. He saw it coming and deflected the blow, then held her hand in his, right there on the street in plain view of the town. A flush of pride and pleasure rushed over her, and she was warm again.

"How about lunch?" Brody asked. "I want to talk to you about a little problem."

"Sure. Is it the same problem you mentioned a couple of weeks ago?"

"Right."

Jessica realized the deputy knew about her. "Oh, are you the one who lives down the road? Brody said there was a deputy close by."

Nick Dorelli admitted he was the one. He led the way into a small deli. When they were settled in a booth, Brody leaned close and told him about the storm last night as well as the shots and the tracks they'd seen on the road.

"A V-shaped cut on the front passenger tire, huh?" The officer got out a notebook and wrote the information down. "I'll keep an eye out." He put the notebook away. "Say, how's my favorite llama doing?"

"My wife has threatened to make llama stew out of my prize breeding stud," Brody complained.

Nick burst into laughter. "Ah-ha, got you with the old green spit trick, did he?"

"Right on my clean shirt," she confessed. Heat seared her breast as she recalled Brody's touch there as he cleaned it off.

Her eyes met his. He remembered, too. And what followed afterward. And last night. A tremor raked through her and her smile became tremulous. She wished they were alone.

Flames danced in his dark eyes, and she knew he was thinking the same thing. She looked down at the table. It was odd to be so in tune with a person, to know his thoughts, to know he knew hers. Did making love do that to a couple?

She met the deputy's eyes, which were as dark as Brody's, and saw his admiration. She realized he approved of her.

After the meal, she picked up her purse and stood. "I have a few items I need to pick up. Where's the nearest drugstore?"

"Around the corner and two doors down." Nick pointed out the window in the direction she should go.

She looked a question at Brody.

"I'll meet you at the store in fifteen minutes."

"Fine. I'm delighted to have met you," she told the deputy, then hurried on her way. She had a feeling Brody was going to talk to Nick and tell him things he didn't tell her. Her husband could be quite maddening when he chose.

Which was most of the time.

As soon as Jessica left the restaurant, Brody and the deputy discussed the storm and its happenings in

greater detail. Brody leaned forward and spoke quietly. "I think the idea was to get rid of me. The perp didn't expect Jessica to come out in the storm, too. I found the gun casing on the ridge. It was hidden but not so it wouldn't be found."

"Sounds like a frame-up," Nick observed.

"Right," Brody agreed. "Now who would want to get rid of me and Jessica and blame it on someone else?"

"The next of kin after the uncle," Nick concluded. "If the uncle is convicted, the will would be overturned."

"My thoughts exactly."

Jessica walked into the drugstore and started looking for the items she needed. At the back of the store, next to the pharmacy area, she paused in front of a rack and studied the advertising on the boxes.

Condoms, it seemed, came in many different shapes and…she gasped…sizes. However did a person know that?

Images flashed into her mind. Her with a tape trying to make Brody let her take his measurements. Him laughing as the size changed before her eyes. The two of them meshed as one, their purpose forgotten in the heat of the moment.

She laid a hand against her chest. Her heart was going as fast as it had last night when he'd held her and driven her mad with the magic of his hands and mouth…

She brought her attention back to the matter at hand. Well, she'd get the large size. That seemed, um, about right.

She didn't think color was important, but what about those ribbed things or the ones with the dangles at the end. No, that looked like a bunch of worms. She suppressed a giggle.

Ah, now here was something interesting.

She read the print on the box with growing amusement. Add fun and excitement to your marriage, the manufacturer advised. Give your significant other a surprise. Impress her with your ardor. She'll know where you are every fun-filled, passionate minute.

Jessica bit her bottom lip to keep from laughing. The condoms were guaranteed to glow in the dark.

She couldn't resist. She dropped the box into her basket, then selected a box of plain ones—in case Brody objected to the glow—and dropped it in with her other items. Then, for good measure—a giggle escaped her—she tossed in the ones with the blue ribbing down the sides.

Brody joined her at the checkout line just as the clerk was dragging her choices over the scanner. The condoms were next.

She felt his quick intake of breath against her arm when he saw the boxes. She met his gaze and, unable to control the mischievous mood, winked.

He gave her a lethal glance, then studied the traffic outside the windows with meticulous attention. His ears were a bit ruddy. One might even say they glowed. Her rugged, supremely masculine, arrogantly confident husband was blushing.

"Very funny," he muttered when they were in the truck and on their way out of town.

She couldn't help it. She burst into laughter. She was still smiling when they reached the ranch.

## Chapter Ten

Brody stopped at the stairs. Jessica nearly ran into his back. She looked at him expectantly.

He realized she was planning on coming up with him. She probably planned on moving in with him...and sleeping with him...and using all three dozen of those damn condoms she'd bought at the drugstore...

A cold sweat broke out on his forehead. It soon turned hot as his body sizzled at the idea of making love to his wife, who was gazing at him with the most innocent expression he'd ever seen on a female's face.

Ha. If she could buy glow-in-the-dark condoms, she wasn't half as innocent as she looked. She was a woman with plans. He knew what they were. She'd entrap him with her charms until he didn't know what was what, then she'd walk out when she'd had enough of the bucolic life...and him.

When the case was solved, she'd hightail it back to the city and her friends there, the charity balls and boozy luncheons—not that Jessica ever drank more than an occasional glass of wine—and all that society junk women loved.

Yeah, he knew how the female mind worked. He'd pleasured her, shown her how good sex could be between a man and a woman. Right now, that was new and exciting. It would pass. Meantime he wouldn't get suckered in.

"Where are you going?" he asked.

She blinked those clear, gray eyes as if she were a sleepy cat, then smiled just as lazily. "With you."

"No way. I like my privacy."

Her expression didn't change. Only her eyes. They opened wider at his announcement, then became a calm, silvery surface that admitted no emotion. He wished he could take the words back so he could see that lazy, sensually content expression again.

She stepped away from the stairs. "Okay."

Going to the guest room tucked under the stairs, she went inside. The door closed behind her.

His frustration level rose to the saturation point. He wanted to break the banister with his bare hands and beat the walls that surrounded him to rubble. Fat lot of good that would do. Maybe he should go on his knees and apologize—

Forget that.

Rubbing the ache that splintered his head, he walked up the stairs, closed the door to his room and went into the office. He placed a call to Denver and checked in with his secretary. He read several pages of faxes, returned calls to a dozen clients or potential clients, then dialed a number in New York.

"Did you get a copy of the grandmother's will?" he asked.

"Yeah, I got it," the attorney responded. "You were right. Everything belongs to Jessica. Judge Parker, who was the executor and prime trustee for Jessica before his death, wrote the grandmother's and the mother's wills."

"You know what I'm thinking, don't you?"

"Yes."

There was a tense ten second silence. "You know what to do if anything happens to either or both of us," Brody directed in a tone of deadly quiet. "You got my instructions?"

"Right."

When Brody hung up, he sat in the executive chair, his hands behind his head, his eyes half-closed as he stared out the window at the snowy peaks of the mountains. He knew for sure who wanted Jessica out of the way. Now he had only to prove it.

And soon.

If his passionate wife was pregnant, no court in the country would let a will stand that excluded her child as an heir. The grandfather was right. Her mother had written a stupid will that meant nothing but trouble for the daughter. He wondered if her attorney had tried to make her see the light…or if he'd been influenced by another family member, and maybe a sweet little packet under the table.

Money. It did strange things to people. In his years of private investigating, he'd seen supposedly close-knit families torn apart by greed or resentment that one sibling had gotten more than another.

He pushed himself out of the chair. Time to see

about the cattle and the ranch chores. Then he'd check the perimeter area.

Jessica didn't know it, but he had security devices planted at every location leading into the ranch. He would know if anyone came in by vehicle. If they came by horse, they might slip through his net, so he kept an eye on the trails, too.

He'd also know if his independent-minded wife tried to leave without telling him.

Jessica glanced up when Brody came in. The sky was dark outside and had been for an hour. She didn't ask where he'd been, though.

He passed her with a nod of greeting but without speaking and went upstairs. She heard the water come on in his shower. In ten minutes, he returned, dressed in a fresh jogging suit, his dark hair still wet.

Leaning against the counter, he watched her cook their dinner. She was preparing a quick meal tonight. Pasta with a light garlic-tomato sauce and a salad would be it.

Ignoring his moody presence, she slipped sourdough rolls into the oven to let them brown. "Dinner is almost ready. Shall we call Don and have him over?"

"No. He eats only soup when he's sick."

"What about the students?"

"They're up with the sheep."

"Oh, that's right." She set the table. He opened a bottle of red wine and poured them each a glass.

She couldn't believe they'd gone back to being these cool strangers. Not after last night.

The icy patch returned to her heart and settled in. She couldn't think of anything to say. She removed the rolls from the oven and dumped them into a napkin-

lined bowl. The pasta went into a bright red one. She retrieved the salads from the refrigerator and plunked the plates on the table.

"It's ready," she announced.

The silence was oppressive during the meal.

"The weather is supposed to be clear for a week," Brody finally said, already half-finished with his pasta and salad. He hardly glanced at her.

"How nice." She swallowed a bite of penne that seemed to swell in her throat as she tried to get it down. If she'd been a crying person, she'd have felt like weeping. She forced herself to eat, bite after choking bite. And keep a pleasant mien.

Her thoughts roamed to the past and the men who had been part of her life. They had all hurt or disappointed her somehow, right up to the present. Poor little rich girl, she chided as she grew more introspective.

They had almost finished before she stopped her internal brooding and spoke. "My father was killed in an auto accident in a winter storm."

Brody gave her a quizzical glance as if he couldn't figure out what had induced that conversational gambit.

"He was supposed to have been at a business conference, but he went to a resort in the Adirondacks with another woman. She was an attorney in his office, a law student studying for the bar exam actually. As a teenager, I never understood how he could do that to my mother...to us."

Brody stopped eating and watched her.

"Mom almost married another man a few months later, but she broke it off. I never did find out why. Kids often don't, but they hear whispers and abruptly stopped conversations, and they worry. For years I've wondered why my mother said I had to marry to take control of my money, considering her past.''

"Maybe she thought her experiences had soured you on men and marriage,'' Brody suggested.

She shook her head. "As a child, I was angry at my father for dying. As a teenager, I hated him for going off with another woman. I'd thought their marriage was perfect. Kids want to believe that. At the very least they accept the flaws in their family as the norm. For them it is. When I was older I decided it was wrong to judge others by my father's actions. I didn't know the dynamics of my parents' marriage.''

"Very wise of you.'' He didn't hide the sardonic overtone.

"What I'm trying to tell you is that I don't expect anything from our marriage.'' She gave him an unflinching perusal. "So you don't have to worry that I'll start making demands because of what happened last night. I know it didn't mean anything.''

To her surprise, guilt flashed over his face, and something that looked like fury. There were other emotions, too, but they were too fast for her to read. But the guilt she recognized.

It rather surprised her, but she'd known Brody was a man of honor when it came to his word, whether in his job or in his personal dealings with another. That was why she'd trusted him in spite of his warnings not to trust anyone. That he also had a conscience regarding the male-female relationship was a bonus.

He took a deep breath and let it out slowly as if reaching for an inner source of control, again surprising her.

"Then it appears we understand each other,'' he said.

"Yes."

They finished the meal without another word. Brody looked angry. She was merely tired. And sore. And discouraged with life and its cruel uncertainties.

Well, someone was trying to kill her. That was enough to lower the spirits. Her husband regretted making love with her. Another downer. Life was not rosy at the moment.

Brody cleaned up his dishes, refilled his wineglass and went into the living room and turned on the television to the news. Listening to the reporter, she thought there must be disasters happening all over the world.

"To each his own," she said, lifting her wineglass and toasting her own feelings of doom.

After straightening the kitchen, she went to her room, showered and put on cotton pajamas and a short matching robe.

She lingered there, unsure what to do. Finally she got out a romance novel in which the heroine had been sent to live with the wicked guardian, who turned out to be the hero once she got past his surly ways.

Jessica wondered if she could get Brody to read the book. There was a lesson for him in it. She finished the story at eleven and prepared for bed. She wondered if her grouchy husband had retired yet. Ranchers usually went to bed early because they got up at the crack of dawn.

Just as she was turning back the covers to climb in, there was a knock at the door. Instead of calling out, she crossed the room and opened the door. Brody stood there.

His eyes seemed so very dark and deep and mysterious. Her heart jumped, then beat furiously as he abruptly moved.

Brody stooped and hooked one arm behind her knees and the other behind her back as he hoisted her off the floor. He was relieved when she didn't tell him to drop dead or hit him with something. He turned and headed up the steps.

"We'll move your things up tomorrow," he said.

"This might be an entanglement," she warned.

That one sassy eyebrow hiked up and mocked him and his guilt and all those other feelings he couldn't define.

He nodded grimly and entered his—their—bedroom. "It's already that."

She looped an arm around his neck and snuggled into his embrace. "What made you change your mind?" Her eyes were bright with curiosity.

"I missed you." That was as much as he was going to admit.

She beamed at him and ran her hands over his chest and his abdomen when he set her on her feet beside the rumpled bed. He was already erect and ready for her.

"Do you often go calling on people in the middle of the night in your, ah, birthday suit?"

"Only when it's you."

He unbuttoned the pretty lavender pajamas she wore and pushed the top off her arms. It fell to the floor. The elasticized bottoms were a simple matter, too. When she was naked—the way he liked her best—he gave in to the desire to let his gaze roam over her at will.

"My God, you're beautiful," he murmured. He sat

on the bed and looped his arms around her hips. She caressed his shoulders.

When he opened his legs, she stepped inside the V of his thighs and pressed close, showing him in ways better than words that she wanted him, too. He knew as long as she stayed with him he wasn't going to try to shut her out again. She was more than any sane man could resist.

Slipping a hand behind her head, he urged her mouth to his, needing the taste and feel of her the way a dying man needs succor.

She responded fully, with her mouth and tongue and hands and body returning every caress of his. When he left her lips and roamed down her breasts, she rubbed her hands through his hair and down his back. Shifting slightly, she rubbed her thigh against him, nearly blowing his mind as red-hot need flashed through him as if it were wildfire.

He lay back on the bed and, hands at her waist, lifted her to the bed so she was on her knees. She gave a soft exclamation of shock when he pressed his face intimately into the springy mound of hair.

He explored her thoroughly while satisfaction stole over him. He was selfish enough to be glad he was the first to show her the full possibilities of pleasure between male and female and arrogant enough to think he'd made it as good for her first time as it could possibly be. He'd make it better this time.

"Brody," she whispered, her voice strained with the passion he built in her. "Brody, I think…"

"Shh," he told her. "Don't think."

"I'm going to fall…"

He felt the tremor rush over her and knew she was close to completion. He reluctantly backed off. Turning them, he let her fall onto the mattress and rest a few minutes while he fondled her breasts. He saw her eyes go to the lamp he'd left on low. It had been pitch-black in the cabin last night.

"Do you want it off?" he asked.

"I don't know." She gave him a helpless smile. "I don't think I like you seeing me disheveled—"

He chuckled. "Now there's a city slicker word if I ever heard one."

"All right, panting and sweaty and out of my mind from what you do to me."

He shouldn't have been, but he was surprised by her total candor. It was a rare trait in a woman, he was pretty sure. At least, he hadn't encountered it often. But she was different. He'd known that from the first moment, the moment he should have run but hadn't.

"Why not?" he asked. "That's what you do to me."

"You seemed in control last night," she reminded him. "I was the one shaking and carrying on like a banshee."

"Last night I had to be careful."

"But tonight you don't?"

He almost laughed at the avid sexual curiosity in her catlike eyes and the earnestness of her question. "Yes, but not as much as last night. I can go a bit wild myself tonight."

The thought raced through his blood like champagne. He'd let her rest long enough. It was time to take her higher.

He began at her mouth again and worked his way down until she cried out and tugged at his hair. He nudged between her legs, then remembered. "Where are the boxes?"

"What boxes?" Jessica was too far gone to remember anything beyond the last five seconds.

"The condoms."

"I threw them in the trash."

He groaned and moved away from her. "Where?"

"The kitchen."

He kissed her once, hard, then padded out. "Don't go 'way," he advised with a mock scowl.

She took several deep breaths to calm her racing heart while he was gone. It did no good. Her heart took off again when he returned. He dumped the three boxes in a drawer, selected one and prepared himself to come to her.

When he realized she was watching, he faced her so she could see his actions. His dark eyes expressed amusement.

"I'll let you do the next one," he promised.

"Okay." She willed herself not to be shy. Brody was her husband, a very considerate husband. Sex was new to her, but it was natural and wonderful. She'd lied when she said it didn't mean anything. She knew differently.

"Entanglements," she said, aware of the icy patch that lingered in her heart.

Brody returned to her. Lying beside her, he trailed a finger over her tummy and circled her navel. "Yes." He bent and kissed her, then started the process of seduction all over again.

This time she watched while he merged their bodies. She decided she liked seeing what was happening and told him so.

"The possibilities are endless," he assured her, his eyes alight with humor and passion.

She thought maybe they were. And the future? Maybe it was endless, too.

Brody breathed the pure air of the mountains and let the sense of well-being pervade his senses. It was a false one, but for the moment, all was well.

"This is beautiful, Brody," Jessica called out behind him.

He twisted in the saddle and watched her lean forward as her mount climbed the last few feet. He'd put her on a gentle gelding, but he saw he needn't have been so cautious. His wife had a natural seat, and she'd ridden often enough to be comfortable in the saddle.

His body stirred.

She was a spirited and natural lover, too, everything a man could ask for in a partner. She did whatever he did to her and experimented on her own to find out more about what he liked. The problem was he liked everything she did.

He quelled the tumultuous passion. This wasn't a good time for her, she'd told him four days ago.

"I'm not pregnant," she'd said, lifting her orange juice glass. She'd gestured as if making a toast, her smile mocking his worry about a child and the entanglements it would create.

Well, hell, it would.

The funny thing was…this was really weird…but he'd felt sort of…well, like he might have been maybe a little disappointed at the news. It had startled him. He'd never considered having a child before.

Gazing at the three thousand acres of land that were his, he realized he had no one to leave it to. Well, there was Carly and Jonathan and the new baby when it came, but they didn't need any money. He would leave everything to a scholarship fund.

He hadn't even written a will. That was stupid. But people were like that, Sloan Carradine, his Denver attorney, had assured him the last time he'd stopped by the law office. Sloan had a wife and a couple of kids now and was obviously content.

Being married made a man think of the future and the responsibilities it might bring. And the possibilities.

"Brody, look, you can see the clouds forming."

He followed his wife's pointing finger. As the warm mid-May air lifted to flow over a nearby mountain peak, the moisture in it condensed into a cloud before their eyes. He'd seen the phenomenon many times and no longer noticed.

Not so with Jessica. She had pointed out each wildflower and sparkly rock and natural occurrence on the trail.

He pushed the thoughts to the back of his mind and concentrated on the trail ahead. He'd spotted tracks up this way earlier in the week. He wanted to see if there were any fresh ones. So far he hadn't seen any.

He wasn't worried about an ambush. The hired gun was cagey and careful in his moves, using the cover of storms and darkness for his deeds. That was why he hadn't hesitated about bringing Jessica on the trip when she'd requested it that morning.

Besides there was a place he wanted to show her. The Rockies were a young mountain range and still forming. That meant there were plenty of hot spots in them. Water, running through the fissures in the earth, seeped into basins of rock, forming pools. Cowboys' bathtubs, they were called. That's where he was taking Jessica.

"A fern meadow," she sang out when they entered a glen where wild ferns unfurled their long leaf spikes.

He nodded and led them down the incline and up another hill. There, he veered off on a narrow path among a forest of pines. The trail wound down the mountain and became gentler in slope but rockier in terrain.

At last they reached the spot where water burbled out the side of a rocky face and tumbled into a mossy pool. The faint scent of sulfur blended with the balsam scent of pines.

"This is marvelous," Jessica said with awe in her tone. "Utterly charming."

"You ain't seen nothin' yet," he teased. He dismounted and left the rein dangling on the ground, then went to Jessica.

Jessica sighed contentedly when he smiled up at her. He held up his arms for her. She tumbled into them. He held her for a second before sending her on her way to explore with a pat on the fanny.

"I'll see to the horses," he murmured.

Hugging her arms across her chest, she walked to the pool and peered into its clear water. When she trailed her fingers in it, she started in surprise. "It's warm."

Brody squatted beside her. "Yeah. It's a natural hot spring. Even in the dead of winter, it's usually warm enough to bathe in."

"Really?" She sounded like a kid just discovering life.

"Yes, really," he mocked. He sounded like a man who desired his wife and wasn't sure he would be welcome.

Four nights with her in his arms but without making

love had put a strain on him. He didn't think he could hold out much longer, especially with her looking at him with something similar to adoration in her eyes. He sucked in a calming breath, but it didn't do any good.

"I brought lunch," he said to distract himself.

She glanced up with a pleased smile. "That was thoughtful."

She said things like that, complimenting and thanking him and Don and the cowboys for little things. Finishing school talk, he called it. He once would have shied from any woman who did that, thinking she was too highfalutin for his tastes. With Jessica, it was different.

Maybe it was because she seemed sincere. It made a man want to do more to win one of her smiles and accolades. Then, too, she always acted surprised when anyone did anything for her. As if she weren't used to servants at her beck and call. Except for the three years she taught in a missionary school in Africa.

His do-gooder wife. He recalled the shine of tears in her gray eyes when he'd brought her a wild rose he'd found growing in the fence row of the horse paddock that morning. He wondered why that would make her cry.

He rubbed his hand down her shiny curls, unable to control the need to touch her. Her hair had grown longer in the six weeks they'd been living at the ranch. It curled over her collar, and the darker color was showing at the roots. Normally she would have had a touch-up by now if she lived in the city. She hadn't once asked to go to town.

"Do you miss city life?" he asked.

She shook her head. "I love it here. I feel free."

When she glanced at him to see if he understood, he nodded. He did. It was the same with him. He dropped his hand and went to get their lunch out of the saddlebags before he did something really stupid. Like make love to her on the spot.

He groaned as his body grew rock-hard in anticipation. The most fleeting thought of her produced the same result no matter where he was. He should be used to it.

When he returned with a blanket and the sandwiches, she had her shoes off and her jeans rolled up to her knees.

"Oh, it's wonderful. Take your boots off," she invited. "You'll love it."

He dropped the blanket behind them, laid the lunch out and yanked off his boots and socks. He wore Western jeans, which were tight in the legs to fit inside his boots.

"Take them off, too," she challenged with a wicked grin when he couldn't get them up past his mid-calf.

Gazing into her eyes, he stood and with deliberately slow motions, unhooked his belt and pants. He peeled them off while her face changed to that hazy glow of passion he'd come to know as well as himself.

He settled beside her, set his feet in the warm water and picked up a sandwich. "Tuna salad with pickle relish," he announced. "Don made them. There're chips and cookies, too."

"And apples." She helped herself.

The silence wafted around them, and the somnolent drone of nature took over, the cadence of bees among wildflowers, the rustle of the wind in the tops of the trees, the murmur of the spring water tumbling over the granite. He ate, but he couldn't take his eyes off her.

"Brody?" she at last questioned.

"Shh," he said. "Just let me watch you."

Pink rose in her cheeks. He didn't understand how she could be so beautiful and so unaware of it. What was wrong with the men in her life that she hadn't been snapped up long ago?

He realized where that line of thought was taking him. Theirs wasn't a real marriage, he reminded himself savagely. As a husband, he'd been bought and paid for in order to keep her safe from her enemies for as long as she needed him.

He'd do that. With his life, if need be.

"Can we swim in the pool?" Jessica asked, jarring him out of his fiercely protective thoughts.

"Yes."

She was on her feet as soon as she stuffed the last bite of sandwich into her mouth. She had stripped by the time she'd chewed and swallowed.

"Last one in is a rotten egg," she declared and stepped up on a boulder, ready to leap.

He caught her around the waist and hauled her back to terra firma. "Not so fast."

Still holding her, he managed to get his shirt and shorts off while she squirmed and fought and tickled him. Then he slipped his hands under her buttocks and walked into the water with her feet dangling at his ankles.

"My feet are in the water." He peered past her and looked down. "Nope, just as I thought. Yours aren't. Now who's the rotten egg?"

Jessica was enchanted. Brody in a playful mood was so rare and new to her that she thought her heart would expand right out of her chest. His interesting features changed with his smile into stunning good looks. His teeth were brilliantly white against his skin, which had tanned to deeper shades of bronze during their six weeks at the ranch.

He walked deeper into the pool. The water came up to their knees, their thighs, their waists, then their necks when he found the ledge and sat down with her in his lap.

She saw his eyes survey the area in his usual alert fashion. She ran her hands into his hair and pulled his face toward hers. Then their lips met.

The kiss was searing at the first touch. He let her explore his mouth first, then he took over, thrusting against her tongue in sensuous play. His hands caressed her breasts until the nipples rose in hard little points of desire.

They kissed and tickled and engaged in all the tricks of a lover's trade for a long time.

Finally his hands moved along her body into more intimate stroking. "Are you all right?" he asked, mumbling the words while he nibbled on her earlobe.

She'd never discussed her personal body functions with a man, but she knew what he meant. She'd been blessed with brief, pain-free menses. "Yes."

His chest lifted as he drew a deep breath. "Then shall we see what new venues we can discover?"

The seductive question sent the blood sparkling through her body as if it were pure champagne. It went right to her head.

"Yes." She could barely whisper the word.

He shifted her across his thighs. "It should be safe now, don't you think?" he asked before he adjusted her on his hard staff. At her nod, he guided her down on him.

They spent the next two hours exploring the possibilities of making love in the warm, swirling water. She thought they'd discovered all of them by the end of that time. She expressed this thought to Brody.

"We'll return soon and make sure," he suggested with a wicked gleam in his eyes as he did enchanting things to her with his hands and the glide of his body against hers.

It occurred to her that she'd never been happier in her life. At the same instant, she knew why. She was in love.

## Chapter Eleven

"Wait here," Brody said when they climbed out of the pool.

Jessica feasted on the sight of his masculine good looks—the broad shoulders, the muscular back, the slender shanks and long, tapering legs—as he went over to his horse and retrieved a towel from the saddlebag. She shivered with emotion as she realized he'd planned this whole scene.

Her heart soared. He was passionately gentle in his lovemaking. He was protective and caring in a way she'd never experienced from others in her life, except maybe her grandmother and that had been so long ago, she barely remembered.

A woman could do worse in a mate.

Of course he was also stubborn and bossy, but as his aunt Essie might have said, a smart woman could handle that. A smile pushed its way onto her mouth. She wrapped her arms across her chest and let the sun stroke her with its warm rays. She was warm all the way through.

She laughed and threw her arms up toward the impossibly blue sky. Brody shook the towel out and slung it over his shoulder. He returned to her, a smile on his face. "What's so funny?"

"Us. This." She gestured around the glen. "A year ago, could you have imagined yourself standing here, as naked as the day you were born, basking in the sun?"

"A year ago, no, but for the past couple of months it's all I've thought about."

Her breath strangled in her throat as she realized the implications. "Have you ever had another—" She stopped. She had no right to ask questions about his past.

"Another woman up here?" He finished the sentence for her.

She nodded.

"Never."

"I'm glad." She leaned against his bare chest and wrapped her arms around him. "I'm selfish where you're concerned. I want you all to myself."

"I'll be a faithful husband," he assured her laconically. "For as long as we're married, you won't have to worry."

She nodded, her mood switching from expansive to pensive. Maybe the marriage would last a lifetime. Brody seemed to enjoy it now. But all men were probably attentive during the early days of making love.

He dried her back, then shifted so he could dry her front. He lingered on her breasts and finally sucked at her nipples.

"Um, sore," she murmured.

His smile flashed in apology. "Sorry, I couldn't resist." He finished and left her to dress while he dried and pulled his clothing on. A cloud drifted over the sun.

"It's clouding up," she commented when they were mounted and ready to start on the trek to the ranch house.

He glanced at the sky. "Nothing to worry about. It might shower on those peaks, but the rain won't reach the valley."

She kept an eye on the storm on the way down, wondering how Brody knew these things. He appeared to be right. The clouds came no farther than the high peak and were left behind as their horses ambled along. When they reached smoother ground, Brody clucked his tongue and both horses swung into a fast walk.

A little after three o'clock, they came out on the ridge above the ranch headquarters. "Home," she murmured. "How very beautiful it is."

The spring grass was thick and green from the rains they'd had. The cottonwoods had leafed out along the creeks that meandered across the pastures. The place exuded serenity. With Don in the hills with the sheep and the students checking fences and moving cattle in the back acres, not a soul was around.

She spotted the two extra horses in a paddock next to the llamas. Brody kept six horses, she'd discovered. The students were riding the other two.

"That's the only reason they work for me, so they can ride horses and think they're real cowboys," he'd explained the other morning after the two young men had left the house.

Jessica had invited the cowboys over for Sunday

breakfast. They had eaten an amount that boggled her imagination…and she was used to cooking for Brody. The biscuits and gravy had disappeared so fast she'd prepared pancakes to make up for the shortage and fried another pound of sausage while they scraped out the bowls.

"The boys will be in early tonight so they can hit town before the loggers take over the saloon. Can you have supper ready by five, five-thirty?"

"Sure. Let's grill steaks. I can toss potatoes in the microwave to bake and make a salad."

"Good." He led the way down the steeply slanting bluff.

She couldn't keep her eyes off her very intriguing husband. He rode with the ease of long experience, his gaze ever restless as he checked the trail and the woods on the right of them. She heard a strange sound, a sort of angry buzz, then her gelding snorted and lunged so abruptly she hadn't time to prepare.

Her feet slipped from the stirrups. She lost her grip on the reins. She grabbed at the saddle horn, but it didn't help. She and the horse were both going over the ledge. The horse screamed. That was the last thing she heard. Pain exploded in her head. The world went dark.

Brody jerked around, not sure what had caught his attention. He saw Jessica's mount rear up, then they both went crashing over the edge of the incline. He leapt from the horse. For the next two minutes, he alternately cursed and prayed as he pulled his rifle from its scabbard and fired several regularly spaced shots into the woods.

He now knew what had caught his attention. The

hiss of a bullet fired from a gun with a silencer. He reloaded the rifle, tucked his handgun into the waistband of his jeans and dropped over the slanted rimrock to see about Jessica.

She lay on her back, one arm outflung as if reaching for something to cling to as she fell. He didn't let himself think of anything but getting to her as he picked his way over the rocks. She turned to her side and curled her legs toward her chest. He breathed freely for the first time since she'd fallen.

He stooped beside her. "Jessica, honey, you all right?" He ran his hands over her arms and legs, then her ribs and collarbone, all the areas of the body he knew were the most vulnerable to breakage. He didn't find the rough ends of splintered bone under her skin, so that seemed okay.

"Honey, can you open your eyes?"

He wanted to haul her into his arms, but he knew better than to move her yet. He checked the rim above them in case their visitor had decided to finish them off then and there. His horse was skittish around strangers. It would snort and dance if anyone came close.

She opened her eyes and gazed up at him. "Hurt," she mumbled. Blood ran out the corner of her mouth.

His heart jackknifed. "Where? Tell me where you're hurt. Don't go to sleep," he warned when her eyelids drooped.

"Head. Shoulder. Arm."

"What about your neck? Can you lift your head?"

She rolled her head back and forth on the wide flat ledge where she lay, then lifted it a half inch. "Yessss." She didn't seem aware that she drawled the word into a hiss. Her eyes closed again.

"Stay alert," he ordered. "We've got to get you out

of here and to a doctor. Jessica? Open your eyes, honey. Dammit, don't you pass out on me, you hear?"

But she didn't. She didn't rouse at all when he prodded her arm. He could hear her breathing. It was shallow and swift. Her pulse seemed to skip every other beat. He clamped the useless curses inside and looked toward the gelding.

The horse was trying to get to its feet, but its hind parts wouldn't move. Brody walked over and spoke soothingly as he assessed the damage. The horse gazed at him trustingly. He'd had it since it was born, had trained it himself to the saddle.

But this horse would never be ridden again. Its back was broken. Still talking in low crooning tones, he put it out of its misery. Heaving a grim breath, he returned to Jessica. She hadn't stirred a hair at the shot.

"Come on, baby, we've got to get out of here."

He hoisted her into his arms and as gently as possible descended the steep slope using the slanting layers of limestone as a walkway, moving down to the next layer when he reached a dead end. Jessica was like a doll in his arms, her head and arms bobbing with each step. At the meadow, he hugged her close, let out a piercing whistle that would bring his horse down to the stable and headed for the sports ute.

He folded the seats down to make a bed, then laid Jessica in it. He ran inside for a blanket and pillows. After covering her and cradling a pillow on each side of her head, he headed out. An hour later, he pulled up at the emergency entrance of the hospital. He'd used the truck phone to call ahead. The medics were ready when he stopped. He followed the stretcher inside.

"How is she?" he asked when a doctor who had

one of those cherubic faces that made him look about thirteen straightened from his examination.

"She's alive," he said and barked out orders to several nurses for IV setups and other equipment.

Brody clenched his hands to keep from pounding the young medic. "How badly is she hurt?"

The doctor turned to him. Brody saw that his eyes were those of a man who'd seen too much in too short a time. "What happened to her?"

"Her horse fell over a cliff. She was on him at the time."

The doctor nodded. He'd heard and seen worse. "She has a concussion. I'm calling in a specialist."

"Get the best," Brody ordered. "I want the best. I can afford it," he added.

The doctor snorted and walked over to the central station. He put in a call.

Brody took Jessica's hand. It was warm. There were small calluses forming on her palm, the result of the ranch work she insisted on doing. She seemed to actually enjoy helping muck out the stalls and hand-feed the orphaned lambs and calves. She'd cut her nails short and tried milking the cow under Don's supervision. She'd actually squeezed a thin stream of milk into the bucket. The cowboys had whooped and applauded. She'd taken a bow, a big grin on her face.

He shook his head. His city slicker wife was a good sport. He bent over her, disturbed by her stillness and by the tubes snaking into her mouth and nose. Ah, God...

"We're taking her to an ICU," the doctor told him, returning to Jessica. He barked out more orders over the noise of an arriving ambulance.

Jessica's injury wasn't an accident. Someone was

trying to kill her. If they'd succeeded, would they have come for him? He would have liked to laid low and found out. If Jessica hadn't been seriously injured, he would have set up a little ambush of his own. But she came first.

The hospital staff tried to make him wait outside, but he stayed with her, leaning against the wall while the specialist was there, then holding her hand after the doc's orders had been carried out. Jessica was packed in ice to control the swelling. If that didn't stop it, they would open her skull next.

He called two of his best detectives and pulled them off other cases. There was one driving thought in his mind—catch the attacker and get the evidence needed to arrest the two-faced jackal behind the crime. He gave out orders, spoke to his secretary, then sat by Jessica's side.

Midnight came, then the gray of morning. She didn't rouse or move once during the night. Her hand, when he touched her, was as cold as glacier ice. So were her lips. Like the Snow Queen, she was cold all over. He settled in a hard chair and waited.

Jessica became aware of sounds first. Strange voices spoke in the air over her head as if they floated there without being connected to bodies at all. For a long time, she simply lay in the bed and listened, too tired to open her eyes, not interested enough to try. She drew a deep breath—it felt as if it were the first she'd taken in days—and let it out slowly.

Nothing hurt at the moment. Fancy that.

She could remember her head pounding fiercely each time she saw a pinpoint of light move across her eyes. She thought that had something to do with the voices because the light and the pain only appeared when the voices did. Then the light would go away and leave her in peace. This time, when the voices came, the light and pain didn't appear.

The darkness flowed over her, soothing and pleasant. She could feel herself drifting deeper into it. So peaceful. So relaxing. But wait...there was light...at the end of the darkness...

This was confusing. She wasn't sure she wanted to go toward the light. With the light came pain and remembering the terrible thing that had happened...

No, no, this was a different light. A new place... She let herself drift toward it.

*I'm sorry, but there's nothing else we can do.*

*The hell it is. Jessica, wake up. Dammit, wake up.*

*Mr. Smith, please, you're not helping...*

Jessica tried to ignore the voices as she'd done in the past, those hateful voices and their probing light, but that one voice...it called up memories...pleasant memories...laughter...warmth...oh, yes, the warmth.

*Jessica, you listening? We have a deal, a full year, remember? A full year, you hear me?*

She sighed. Really, all this commotion. The light at the end of the darkness blinked out. Panic swept over her. She would lose the way without that light. She tried to see through the darkness but couldn't. She had to—

*Open your eyes. That's an order.*

That maddening, imperious voice. She suddenly knew who it belonged to. And she had a thing or two to say about orders.

She opened her eyes.

"About damn time." Brody glared at her, his face hovering over hers, only inches away.

"Don't yell at me," she told him. Her voice was hoarse, raspy. It didn't come out with the force she'd wanted.

The people surrounding the bed laughed as if this was the funniest thing they'd ever heard. It was obviously they were on his side. She tried to remember what they were arguing about. It was too much effort.

"I'm sorry." He grinned at her, not sorry at all. "How do you feel?"

She thought about it. "Thirsty."

That brought more laughter. These were really strange people. But cheerful. She liked that.

Brody held a straw to her mouth. She sucked a few swallows of water, then rested again.

"Thank you." She laid her head on the pillow and watched him place the glass on the bedside table. "You need a shave."

In fact, he looked terrible. She'd seen him covered with dust from working with the cattle. She'd seen a five-o'clock growth of beard when he came in at the end of the day. She'd seen him with his hair tousled by the wind. But she'd never seen him like this.

His eyes were bloodshot. His face sported a beard that was at least three days old. His shirt looked as if he'd slept in it. There was a spatter of coffee stains down the front.

"I'll take care of it," he promised, rubbing a hand over his jaw. He winked at her.

She tried to smile, but she really was tired now. She yawned, then grimaced as her head started hurting again. There had been no pain in that floating, peaceful darkness, but she instinctively knew she wouldn't find it again.

"I'm going to look at you," a vaguely familiar voice told her. Oh, yes, the doctor. Her memory returned.

"I fell off my horse," she said.

"And over a bluff," Brody confirmed. "You hit your head."

"Is Captain all right?" She couldn't remember the other horses' names, but there were five more.

"He's fine," Brody assured her.

"Good." She let the doctor look into her eyes with his annoying little flashlight. Then she went to sleep.

The next time she awoke, it was Brody's voice again that prodded her to wake up.

"Breakfast," he said when she looked at him.

An aide brought a tray for her and one for Brody. She studied the Cream of Wheat and dish of Jell-O, then peered at Brody's tray. He had a thick round of Canadian bacon, a mound of scrambled eggs, two biscuits and a roll, plus juice and coffee.

"I'll have what he's having," she told the woman, really miffed at the discrepancy in food.

The aide checked the menu chart. "Um, it says you're on a light diet."

Jessica accepted the inevitable and thanked the woman as graciously as she could. She stole another glance at Brody.

He was clean-shaven. His hair was neat, and he wore a white shirt with the sleeves rolled up and a pair of navy slacks. Except for the missing coat and tie, he looked very much as he had when they'd first met.

Including the same all-business manner and an identical scowl on his face.

On the ranch, she found a different side to her taciturn husband. That he could laugh. That he was caring toward his hired hands and his animals. That he was gentle.

She sighed as a depression settled over her. She didn't know why she was sad, but she was. She remembered the cold that had encased her in the darkness and shivered.

"Here," Brody said when the aide had bustled out after raising the bed and moving the tray table within reach. He brought his food over and forked a bite of egg into her mouth. "Nobody could eat that pap."

He shared his breakfast with her.

She shook her head after a few bites, refusing more. "My eyes were bigger than my tummy," she told him.

"You haven't eaten in four days."

"Four? I've been asleep for four days?"

He met her startled gaze solemnly. "You were unconscious for three and a half days. Your sleep was normal last night, or so the doctor said."

She put her fingers to her temples.

"How's the head?"

"Better. It hardly hurts at all. That's all I recall—that my head hurt terribly, and it got worse when someone shined a light in my eyes."

She stole a biscuit and broke it in half before he wolfed it down. He'd almost finished with his meal. He buttered her half, then his, and added jelly to both.

"You didn't react to the light."

"It was too much trouble." She munched on the biscuit and found it very good. "I was so cold."

He picked up his coffee cup. "You were packed in ice for forty-eight hours." He took a drink.

She noticed his hand trembled slightly. "Oh. Everything seemed so strange. Tell me, what have you been doing for the four days I was sleeping my head off?

And when do I get to leave? I got a real hankering for home," she said in her best John Wayne drawl.

Emotion, too fleeting to be read, flicked over his face. "I'll ask the doctor about discharging you. As for what I've been doing, I've been sitting here on my can waiting for you to wake up, lazybones. Don and the cowboys said to tell you they've missed you." He scarfed the last bite of biscuit and started on the sweet roll.

She snorted indignantly. "I know what you men miss when a woman isn't around. The cooking."

He polished off all but the last swallow of milk and offered it to her. She drank it. He set the glass on the tray and pushed the table away. He half laid on the bed, his elbows on either side of her.

"There were other things I missed," he told her, his voice dropping to a husky baritone. He smoothed the hair from her temples, then cupped her face. His mouth touched hers, once, twice, a third time.

"Well, I'd say you were feeling better."

Brody moved away when the doctor stopped by her bed. Jessica studied the young man's face. He looked like a friend's younger brother, one just entering puberty. "Were you a child prodigy?" she asked.

He laughed. "Don't let this pretty face fool you. Inside beats the heart of a mad surgeon. This guy wouldn't let me operate on your brain. I wanted to take it out and see if I could figure out what made women tick." He nodded toward Brody. "Some watchdog you got there."

She smiled at her husband. The peace she'd found in the darkness returned. Yet, there were other troubling things. She tried to think, but couldn't bring them to mind.

"When can I go home?"

"In a couple of days. If you promise to stay off horses for the next eight weeks. Also, no choppy boat rides. Um, no high speed chases. No bungee jumping, parachuting…"

She was laughing by the time he reached the end of his list. "What about normal activities?" She glanced at Brody, thinking of their nights together and his exquisite lovemaking.

"You'd better give it another week, then start in slowly." He beamed at her, then Brody, then back to her. "No marathon housecleaning for a month. Easy does it." He slipped her chart under his arm, shook her hand and left them.

Jessica grimaced in disgust. She could feel the heat in her face. When she looked at Brody, he was wearing a big grin.

"Was I that transparent in what I was thinking?" she demanded.

He leaned over her again. "Only to a close observer."

He touched her breast. The nipple jutted against the hospital gown as if it were a little peg. She groaned in embarrassment.

"Now where were we before we were so rudely interrupted? Ah, I know." He kissed her again.

When Brody lifted his head, he gazed into her eyes for a long moment. He could feel the bonds of shared experience wrapping around them, drawing them together. The camaraderie of the foxhole was a well-known phenomenon.

And in this case, it was false.

He and Jessica weren't soldiers. He was her hired gun, and so far he'd done a damn poor job of protecting her. The man had slipped past his network of security devices without triggering any of them.

"I'll do better by you," he promised.

The one eyebrow he had learned to observe for an indication of her temperament rose in question. He couldn't explain what had happened. He didn't think she was ready for the truth yet. But it was only a matter of time before they would know for sure who was behind the attempts on her life.

Her lips curled upward in amusement. "If you do much better, I really will die, right in your arms," she suggested with engaging innuendo. She dropped her lashes to a sexy level while laughter hovered in her eyes.

His heart clenched as if a giant hand had reached inside and squeezed it to the bursting point. He'd protect her, this woman he'd come to know as brave and true, with his life.

"Why the frown?"

"Just thinking," he said.

"Hmm, it's really hard on you, I see."

He feigned a jab to her chin and lingered to caress the smooth flesh. "Show some respect for your betters, woman."

"I will. When I meet them."

"Watch it. Falling on your head turned on your true smart-mouth personality. Maybe I should call the doc back and tell him to go ahead and operate on your brain."

"Huh." The word was a challenge.

Relief swept over him. Her spirit was as plucky as ever. She would be all right, whatever the future held.

"I have some work to do at the office. Can you make it on your own until evening?"

"Of course. I'm going to take a nap." She rolled her eyes. "Can you believe I'm sleepy again?"

He caught the flash of vulnerability in her expression before she smiled prettily and smoothed the sheet, tucking it under each arm as she prepared to nap.

Words caught in the back of his throat. He didn't know what he wanted to say, but they were there, crowding up from some place deep inside. He straightened from the bed and went to the door, reluctant to leave her.

She waved goodbye, then covered a yawn. Her lashes drifted closed. He lingered, something besides words filling his chest, making it tight and achy.

"Hey, chief, I wondered if you were going to leave. I've been here for an hour." Joe Hernandez, one of his best men, was waiting several feet down the corridor.

"Good. Thanks for coming in on your day off."

"No problem."

"Did you or MacPherson find anything more?"

"Yeah. Mac found the casing. It was the same as the one you brought in a couple of weeks ago. The guy makes his own shot, using rock salt as you suspected. That's why there was no mark on the horse."

"I think he was after me this time. I felt the sting on my leg when my mount was hit. Luckily, the gelding didn't panic. Did you find out what happened to the infrared detector?"

"Yeah. He didn't use the trail. He came through the woods. Laid down a track a blind man could follow."

"He's craftier than I thought a city slicker would be."

"Yeah." Joe visually checked out the people getting off the elevator. "He's probably getting a little stressed about messing up. That's not a good image for a professional man. Next time he'll do better.''

"My thoughts exactly. You know how to ride a horse?''

"Me? Sure. I was bustin' broncos for pocket money before I was half grown.''

"How would you and Mac like a job at the ranch for a while?''

"Great. I hear your wife can cook like a dream.'' The private investigator was forever trying to cadge an invitation to a meal with the married men's families.

"She does everything like a dream,'' Brody affirmed.

Joe's eyes opened wide. "Yo, chief, you in love?''

Brody speared the impertinent bachelor with an impatient stare. "Watch your mouth and this room. Anybody gets through to her, you'll be dead.''

The younger man sobered. "Nobody has ever got through me.''

"See that it stays that way.'' Brody strode to the bank of elevators and hustled into one of the cars as the door opened. He impatiently punched the Down button. He had things to do and people to see...actually to call. It was time some of Jessica's family came for a visit.

# Chapter Twelve

Jessica sighed as Brody guided the sports ute around the last bend leading to the ranch house. She couldn't believe how weak she felt after spending five days lounging around because of a blow to the head. Now that she was home, she expected to feel a lot better in no time.

Brody parked right beside the back porch. "Wait," he ordered. He came around and opened the truck door.

"Thank you, kind sir." She laid a hand to her heart as if overcome by his thoughtfulness.

"Get in the house before I conk you on the head for insubordination," he ordered.

She didn't blink an eye at that threat. Instead she put her arm around his waist and leaned into him, drawing on his strength as she gazed over the acres of pasture that dwindled to a narrow gorge in the mountains. The sky glowed azure. The sun massaged her scalp like warm fingers. The breeze caressed her body and toyed with her hair.

"Home," she murmured. "I didn't realize how precious it could be."

Brody cast her an odd look, at once grim, sort of brooding and yet she thought there was tenderness, too. He'd been quiet and withdrawn again the past couple of days, more like when they first met rather than as the lover he'd been those two weeks before her accident.

That reminded her. Her gaze went to the meadow where five horses munched the spring grass. She could see the two young cowboys working on an electric fence over near the creek. Don would be up in the high country beyond the gorge with the flock.

"Where's Captain?" she asked. "I don't see him."

Brody didn't answer.

"I've been trying to figure out what made him rear up like that. Do you think he got stung by a bee? That happened to me one time when I was riding my bike. I had a wreck. Fortunately, the car I nearly mowed over managed to stop before we crashed."

"Were you hurt?" he asked.

She looked up in time to catch the fierce frown on her husband's face. "Not other than the sting and a scraped knee. The bee flew under my blouse and stung me when it realized it was trapped in a strange place. I found its poor little carcass after I picked myself up off the pavement."

"Huh," he said noncommittally.

"Did you move Captain? You didn't say where he was."

Brody laid his hands on her shoulders and turned her

to face him. "His back was broken in the fall. I had to put him down."

Those few minutes of falling through space, the terrified scream of the horse, her own fear as she realized they were going over the bluff, came back to her. Tears welled before she could control them. "I should have known—"

"No. I lied to you at the hospital. I didn't want you to face that the moment you woke. I knew you'd feel guilty." His hands tightened. "It wasn't your fault."

"If I'd been more alert, maybe I'd have seen the bee... Was it a bee?"

Brody shook his head. His expression remained grim.

"Did someone...Brody, I heard something. I remember now. It was close, a sort of pop and hiss. Was it an air rifle or something like that?"

"Yeah, something like that."

"You said the other man used rock salt to stampede the sheep. Was it the same person, do you think?"

He nodded, his eyes never leaving hers. "My men found the salt on the trail where you and the gelding went over."

The brightness went out of her heart. Cold reality set in. "I'm never going to be free. That damned money is going to hang like a curse over the rest of my life...should I live so long."

Her laughter was bitter, the first time he'd ever heard her like that. He let go of her shoulders and slipped his hands down her back. He wrapped his arms around her waist and hugged her close enough to feel her heartbeat.

"You'll live to be a hundred and twenty. I guarantee it."

"How? At the risk of your own life? Let me go, Brody. Let me disappear for a year. Then maybe—"

"Forget that. You'll stay where I can see you."

"Why? I've brought you nothing but trouble. That's all I am—trouble with a capital *T.*"

"Yeah, but I like sleeping with you." He tilted her face up to his. He grinned as he lowered his head.

"Well, there is that," she agreed just before his kiss landed on her mouth.

When he let her up for air, he added, "And the cooking. Don't forget the biscuits and homemade chocolate chip cookies and the cobbler you made last week."

"Mmm-hmm."

He kissed her again. "Waffles and potato pancakes."

By the time he lifted his mouth from hers, her eyes had lost the bitterness and were shining like moonstones.

"I'd never give up those dumplings," he added for good measure.

When she laughed, he guided her into the house and insisted she lie on the sofa while he heated the soup that Don had sent over to help her recover. She smiled over the soup, then her eyes teared up again. His wife was emotionally vulnerable today.

His heart clenched tight. Odd how it kept doing that.


Jessica listened to the music on the CD player and drifted into a doze. She'd been home for five days and felt fine, but Brody, brute that he was, wouldn't let her do a thing. He and Don did all the cooking.

She'd discovered there were two other men on the ranch, both from Brody's agency. She'd never seen them, but Brody had explained their presence.

A shiver chased up and down her spine. Brody expected something to happen soon.

Worry gnawed at her. If something should befall him… It was an unbearable thought. Love joined with anxiety and guilt to form an achy ball in her chest. Each night she clung to him, afraid he would be hurt, unable to voice her fears.

"I'm too mean to kill," he'd scoffed when she'd said something to him about being careful.

"You're flesh and blood," she'd reminded him.

"Come on, Jess, don't be a worrywart."

She'd never been called Jess before. She liked it from Brody. She wouldn't have from anyone else.

Her sleepy thoughts were disturbed by the sounds of a vehicle in the driveway. Yawning, she went to see who it was. The housekeeper had already been there that morning.

She blinked, then blinked again when a man climbed out of a rental car. He was dressed in gray flannel slacks, a blue blazer and an open-throat white shirt. She went out on the porch, raising one hand to shade her eyes.

"Uncle Jesse," she called. "Whatever are you doing here?"

He removed a weekender from the trunk. "I came to see how my favorite niece was faring. Your note saying you were married left several questions in my mind."

"I invited him," another voice said.

Brody stepped on the porch from the side of the house. He stretched out a hand in welcome. The two men shook hands and sized each other up. "Come in," Brody invited.

Hooking an arm around her shoulders, he led the

way inside. Her uncle was shown to the guest room. She and Brody went into the kitchen. She looked a question at him.

"Later," he murmured, stalling her queries. He slid his arms around her and placed a string of kisses along her temple. "How are you feeling today? Headache gone?"

"Yes. I'm totally well."

A light danced in his eyes, causing heat to rise in her. When he looked at her in a certain way, it made her heart jump around in her chest as if it were a deer leaping on all fours into the air.

Her uncle joined them. Brody let her go and moved away. She poured glasses of iced cinnamon tea and served cookies with it. She wondered if she was feeding her enemy.

Ancient tribes used the sharing of food as a sign of truce and peace. It would take more than food to appease her uncle or whoever wanted to do her in. He wanted her money—all of it.

A chill passed over her heart.

Brody glanced at her when she folded her arms across her waist. She forced a smile. It was very discouraging to distrust one's own relatives. Brody was the only person she believed in completely. She even doubted her grandfather these days. He hadn't responded to her note or her calls in the seven weeks of her marriage.

Seven weeks and two days. Almost two months.

"Earth to Jessica," Brody intoned, leaning down and peering into her eyes.

She impulsively kissed him, then tapped his cheek. "I'm here. I was listening instead of talking all the time, as you men accuse women of doing."

"Are you tired? You're supposed to be taking a nap."

"I'm fine. Really."

"Sure?"

"Now who's being a worrywart?"

Her uncle laughed. "I see I can stop worrying about you two and the quickness of your marriage. I can tell you're in love."

"Yes," Brody said in a husky tone. "Very much so."

Jessica drew a careful breath. When she looked at Brody, he was watching her uncle, his gaze unreadable. But she knew her husband now. He didn't say anything without a purpose. He was throwing her uncle plenty of rope. Now they'd have to wait and see if he used it. And what for.

They chatted the rest of the afternoon. Brody grilled steaks while she prepared duchess potatoes and salads. The cowboys took their steaks and ate at Don's house, where they also slept in the bunk room.

At ten, Brody declared it was time for her to be in bed. She'd thought he would stay up and talk to Uncle Jesse in private, but instead he came up with her. As soon as they were in the door, he took her into his arms.

"I hope you don't mind about your uncle being here," he said, a question in the words.

"No, but...why did you invite him?"

His expression hardened. "I wanted to see if he'd show up."

She sighed and laid her cheek against him. She could hear the steady thump of his heart and found it reassuring. "Do you think he'll try anything?"

"He wouldn't dare."

The menace behind the bald statement was frightening. "Don't do anything rash, okay? No showdowns or shoot-outs or anything, you hear?"

He laughed, a deep chuckle that rumbled in her ear as if it were distant thunder. "You've been seeing too many movies while you've been lazing around. Time to put you back to work. And I know the first task you need to perform."

"What?" She leaned her head back and looked up at him.

His hands went to her blouse. He began unfastening it. With his usual efficiency, he peeled her out of her clothes, then did the same on his. "Make your husband happy. It's a woman's job," he advised sanctimoniously.

"Ha." But she proceeded to touch and caress him in all the ways she knew he liked. He did the same for her. Lying in his arms, bathed in contentment, she laughed softly.

"What's so funny?" he demanded. His voice was still husky, but with the urgency gone.

"I was thinking of jobs. I shall have to write a glowing recommendation for you. You definitely go above and beyond the expected for your clients."

His arms tightened. "Not for any client. You're the only one I ever married."

"True." She hesitated. "Thank you, Brody. You've been wonderful to me—"

He kissed her into silence. She bit back the words on her tongue. Brody didn't like emotion.

Jessica breathed in the vibrant May air. "Isn't it wonderful, Uncle Jesse? The air is so clear here, the sky bluer than sapphire. I love it."

"It's pleasant," he conceded.

They stood with their arms propped on the top rail of the pasture fence, the one with cows, not the llamas. Her uncle was dressed in blue linen slacks and jacket this morning with a white T-shirt. He, like her grandfather, looked younger than his age, which was fifty. She didn't want the llama to spit on his chic outfit. She had on jeans and a shirt as usual.

He stuck his hands into his pockets. "You seem happy with your detective husband."

"Yes."

"Life can be disappointing. You think you've found everything you could possibly desire and then *poof!* it's gone."

"Have you broken up?" she asked kindly. He and his partner had been together for years.

"Charles thinks he must have a child to pass on his heritage and worldly goods."

"Why don't you adopt? Or have a surrogate mother like in a movie I saw recently?"

"Please," he murmured with a grimace.

"Well, yes, there could be problems, but you should explore the possibilities before giving up."

"I've never considered it necessary. I had your mother, and then you. I expect I'll also have a grand-niece or nephew soon to leave my riches to." His perusal was sly, but pleased.

Jessica started. She hadn't thought more about a child since she'd discovered she wasn't pregnant. "I'd like a child," she admitted. If she and Brody lived long enough...

Her thoughts solemn, she showed her uncle around the home paddocks, then hiked up to the bluff with him. She wondered if she was being a fool, taking him to a place where he could push her off and simply say it was an accident.

She needn't have worried. Brody appeared on the trail the moment they reached the rimrock ledge. He sat on a boulder and spread his legs, indicating she should sit there and lean against him. She did. He wrapped his arms across her waist and rested his chin on her head occasionally while they talked. His Stetson shaded both of them from the rays of the sun.

The morning passed quite pleasantly. After lunch, she did take a nap while Brody took over the duties as host. When she rose, the men joined her on the porch. Brody served a wine cooler he made specially for her. They watched the sunset.

When they went to bed, she turned to him, anxious for his lovemaking. Each moment might be her last with him. She had to grab each one as it came along.

"Don't," he whispered, touching the frown between her eyes. "Trust me to take care of you."

She cupped his face in her hands. "I trust you with my life, my fortune and my…" She paused while she searched for a substitute for heart. "My sacred honor, as our forefathers would have said."

"And did say. Is sex part of your personal declaration of independence?" He nuzzled her ear, then her throat before moving downward to caress her breasts.

"I don't know. Love me, Brody. Just love me."

As if their lovemaking was life itself, he poured his strength and energy into it, laving her with kisses and caresses until she writhed and cried out in soft murmurs of ecstasy, lost to danger and suspicion, aware only of his hands and mouth and body and of her great love for him.

He would protect her with his life. She would do the

same for him. She held him desperately, not wanting the moment to be over. The future drew near, ominous and threatening. Worry washed over her, bringing an avalanche of fear.

"Please," she whispered, "be careful."

"Always," he assured her. "I'll always be careful with you. That's a promise."

"I can see the attraction," Uncle Jesse said, scanning the impressive peaks surrounding the ranch.

Jessica stared out the window as the sports ute wound higher into the mountains. Brody was driving, her uncle was in the front and she sat in the back.

They were delivering supplies to the mountain cabin. She and Brody would stay while Don and Uncle Jesse returned to the ranch. Don's nephew was due in that afternoon. Brody thought the shepherd should be there to greet his relative.

Her tough husband was thoughtful that way. She let her gaze caress the back of his head. He was wonderful in more ways than she could count. She fell more deeply in love each day.

Love. She hadn't had any idea how potent and exhilarating it could be.

"You're quiet back there," Brody said.

"I'm admiring the view." She ogled him.

His dark gaze met hers in the rearview mirror. A thrill ran over her. His eyes held the promise of passion to come. They'd be alone at the cabin for two nights. Her blood heated and her pulse sped up at the memories that came to mind. Sleeping two to a cot would always occupy a special place in her heart.

Brody smiled lazily, then turned his attention back to the dirt track. They pulled into the long, narrow valley before lunch. The two collies barked a greeting, but didn't leave their woolly charges when the three of them climbed out.

Don shook hands with her uncle, then gave Brody a report on a wild cat that had moved into the gorge at the end of the valley. "It's a male. He's passing through."

She wondered how he knew that, but didn't question him. She'd learned the old shepherd knew the nature of animals and the seasons better than anyone she'd ever met. He'd taught her some of the signs.

The circle she'd seen around the moon last night could indicate an approaching storm. It was caused by moisture, usually ice particles, high in the atmosphere. In spite of the day's warmth, she shivered slightly as she thought of another storm. Someone had tried to kill them the other time she'd been up here.

She searched the perimeter of the woods, wondering what evil lurked in there—

"Here." Brody broke into her thoughts when he hefted a five-pound sack of flour at her.

Distracted, she went inside and put the groceries away while the men unloaded the ute. She discovered Don had a pot of stew on the hot plate for their lunch. She served crusty Dutch rolls she'd made the previous day and glasses of spring water with the meal. Uncle Jesse had made brownies, his one gustatory skill he assured them, and they had those for dessert. He and Don left soon after that.

Jessica waved them off and watched until the truck disappeared. Brody was already checking out the flock. She went over and sat on a boulder.

"It's just you and me, kid," she told him in her best Bogie imitation.

"Yeah." Brody gave her an oblique glance that had her insides tied into knots in a second.

She stood, restless with energy. "Where's Ram?" She peered over the flock. She was surprised that he hadn't come bounding over to cadge a pat and something to eat.

"He might not remember you now that he's been with his own kind for a while. He's probably found some sweet little thing to occupy his mind."

Laughter bubbled in her. "Ah, yes, the call of nature."

"Mmm-hmm," he agreed, his quick glance once more sizzling her insides to cinders.

Ah, love. The things it did to a person.

Brody abruptly strode off. "I'm going to check the gorge for cat tracks. Do you mind staying here and keeping an eye on the sheep?"

"No." She looked at the ewes and lambs. They were grazing or snoozing or just gazing into the distance. The dogs rested nearby, ready for a command to leap into action. "What do I do?"

He grinned. "Sit there and look pretty."

She stuck her hands on her hips. "No problem."

Chuckling at her frown, he offered instructions. "Let them graze. If anything happens, circle your arm and the dogs will round them up and move them in the direction you point or you start moving. Nothing will happen," he added.

"Do I move them to the dip where we went in the storm?" she asked, ignoring his assurance.

"No. You keep them close to the cabin. If anything does happen to frighten you, drop the two-by-four across the door and stay inside until I come for you. There's a handgun on the shelf over the plates. Use it if you have to. Don't come out for anyone but me or Nick Dorelli. No one, got that?"

She nodded. "Got it."

He loaded his rifle and headed toward the end of the valley. She settled on the boulder.

The brightness had gone out of the day. Brody seemed his usual self, but she could sense the tension in him. He'd never spoken of danger so openly to her before. It reminded her of why she'd hired him in the first place and why they'd married.

Living at the ranch with him, sharing a bed and bathroom, eating all their meals together, all the intimate acts that a husband and wife shared had overshadowed the danger. Now it was brought home to her like a slap in the face.

"I hate it," she said to the collie lying nearest her.

It wagged its tail and turned one ear toward her, but its eyes stayed on the flock it guarded.

"Good girl," she said.

As the afternoon wore on, she became sleepy. She stood and ambled around the clearing, her gaze flicking often to the far end of the valley where the land narrowed into the steep gorge of boulders and loose rock that had been carved by aeons of storms.

The valley had been formed by glacier action. Its bowl-shaped sides and fairly level floor told of a past when great floes of ice had pushed through, scouring the land into its present outline. The mighty peaks spoke of volcanic action deep within the bowels of the earth.

For all the evidence of ongoing violence, she felt as one with this land. Here she'd found peace...and all the desires of her heart. The thought of leaving left her chilled to the bone. She wouldn't go, not willingly—

The ring of a shot froze her in place. She began to run, fear a great ache in her chest. She was halfway up the valley when Brody appeared. She threw herself at him.

"Where the hell do you think you're going?" he demanded, not at all pleased.

"Are you all right? I heard a shot." She drew back and checked him over for blood. None was visible.

"I ran across the cat's tracks and followed them. He was eyeing the sheep. I used the gun to kick up a little grit in his face. He hightailed it back up to high country."

"Don't you ever scare me like that again," she ordered, angry at him now that the fear was unnecessary. "You go off and put yourself in danger without a thought to your own mortality. A mountain lion can be as dangerous as a two-footed opponent."

"Yes, ma'am." His smile was sardonic.

She punched him in the stomach. "Did you see any other tracks?"

"No." He caught her wrist and twisted her arm behind her, bringing her in tight against him. "I think you need to be taught a lesson, too."

"You gonna shoot me?" she challenged, mocking his tone.

"No, ma'am," he assured her in his best cowboy drawl. "There's a shady spot about a hundred yards from here that's nice and private. Would you like to see it?"

"Would you like a black eye?" She wasn't appeased.

He looped his arm around her waist and guided her toward the woods. When they were among the trees, he led the way to a hammock of willows. There he laid the rifle aside and made a bed with his shirt. "My lady," he invited, sitting and opening his arms to her.

She couldn't resist. She went down on one knee and pushed him to the ground, then she fell on him and kissed him for all she was worth.

"Wait, I have something," he murmured.

He rolled her off him and onto his shirt, then dug in his pants pocket. He removed three packets and laid them in a neat row on the mossy turf.

"Take your pick," he invited.

"How very considerate of you," she complimented. She gave the decision serious thought. "The one with the blue ribbing. I think." She lingered over the selection, delighting in the play between lovers that was so new to her and enjoying the buildup of anticipation between them.

Brody watched her with amusement dancing in the flames of desire in his eyes. It thrilled her that he wanted her. It touched her that he willingly followed her lead and that he put her pleasure before his. He was, in so many ways, a remarkable man and a most tender husband.

"An excellent choice," he said when she finally decided. He folded her into his arms and laved her with his hot, exciting kisses. She shivered, then sighed, then caught her breath as his caresses became bolder and bolder.

She heard him chuckle, then he, too, grew solemn as they kissed and the magic worked its spell on them. They stayed in the glen for an aeon or two before they remembered the sheep.

## Chapter Thirteen

Jessica yawned contentedly and settled on her favorite boulder. Another rock provided a backrest. She hugged her jacket close and watched the twilight turn the world to pink and magenta. Hints of purple showed in the shadows of the woods.

Brody came out of the cabin. He carried the rifle over and propped it against one of the boulders. In his waistband she saw the butt of a handgun. The evening chill crept inside her.

"Let's walk," she requested.

He narrowed his eyes and surveyed the valley. He watched the dogs for a moment. "All right."

They ambled around the perimeter of the flock. A whistle and a movement of his arm sent one collie off in the opposite direction they walked. The other he motioned to go with them.

She knew the collies would sound a warning long

before the two humans spotted anything in the vicinity. It gave her a sense of security to have them. She felt the same with Brody.

"I wonder where Ram is," she mused aloud when they were about halfway around the meadow. He hadn't come to the cabin to be fed as she'd expected.

Brody smiled. "I think you'll soon know." He nodded to the west where a commotion was going on.

One of the collies had routed a bunch of sheep out of a gully and was driving them back to the main flock. One lamb, smaller than the rest, butted at the dog, then bleated and ran to one of the ewes when the collie dropped his head and snapped at the lamb's heels.

Jessica started laughing. "Oh, yes, still up to his usual tricks, I see." She observed the rambunctious lamb and the ewe for a moment. The lamb still had a patch of wool on his back where Brody had glued some of the ewe's fleece.

Nostalgia made her grow pensive as she thought of the days she'd spent hand-feeding the frolicking little bully. The breeze blew her hair into her eyes. The wind was much cooler now that the sun was completely below the horizon.

Ram threw up his head, uttered a plaintive bleat and raced across the pasture as if pursued by wolves. He leapt into the air and would have struck Jessica in the chest if Brody hadn't moved first. He caught the blur of fleece in midair.

"Hold on, you mangy critter," Brody ordered when the lamb thrashed to be free. "Ouch, dammit."

The hard head connected with Brody's chin.

Jessica laughed until her sides ached as man and beast waged war. Brody set the animal on the ground and held him there while she knelt to pet and caress and make crooning noises. Ram butted her hands the way he used to do when he wanted food or pats.

"He does remember me." She smiled happily up at Brody.

"You'd be a hard woman to forget."

His gaze was pensive the way hers had been earlier. The cold crept down her neck. She wondered if he was thinking of the future and a time when she was no longer here.

"Would you want to forget me?" she asked.

His face hardened, the angular bone structure becoming more prominent as he flexed his jaw. "I might."

The enigmatic answer did nothing to soothe her heart. It came to her that Brody might wish this whole situation to be resolved so they could arrange for the divorce and each of them return to their real lives.

He stood and moved off, leaving her to scratch Ram's hard head and fluffy ears. She swept the area and the dark woods beyond the valley floor with an intent gaze. Usually she saw nothing but quiet beauty. Tonight she saw the danger.

When Ram grew restless, she sent him back to the flock with a swat on his rump and looked around for Brody. He stood nearby.

"Ready?" he asked.

She nodded. He guided her around the flock and sent both dogs ahead of them as they finished their walk.

When they returned to the cabin, he heated water and let her prepare for bed first. While she slipped into a navy sweat suit, he emptied the basin for her.

"I'm going out for a while," he told her. "I want you to stay inside, even if you hear shots." He smiled to show he was joking. "Bolt the door and open it only for me."

"All right."

She didn't tell him to be careful. He always was. She knew he'd checked out the area thoroughly before he took her to the glen that afternoon. He had a duty to protect her. He would never let anything interfere with that.

An hour crept by while she read a romantic suspense novel. Maybe she shouldn't have chosen a book with the heroine being chased by the bad guy, a serial killer whose face she could identify. Her hair stood on end whenever the maniac got close.

Nine o'clock came and went.

She needed to go to the outhouse. Standing at the window, she peered through the deepening twilight. There was still plenty of light to see by. She wouldn't need a flashlight.

Brody wasn't in sight. No one was. It should be safe. He'd have surely told her if he'd seen tracks when he scouted the valley that afternoon. If he had, they wouldn't have spent time in the glen making love.

She turned out the overhead light and slipped out the door and around the cabin as if she were a thief.

In less than two minutes, she headed back for the cabin. She'd taken no more than ten steps before she realized she wasn't alone. Someone was coming right at her. Fast.

"I told you to stay in." Brody loomed into view, moving like a racing shadow.

"I didn't see you lurking there in the dark," she accused, rubbing her arms where goose bumps rippled.

"You wouldn't have seen anyone else, either," he said in a snarly tone.

"I had to go to the bathroom." She groaned internally. She sounded like a petulant child.

"I told you not to come outside." He bit off a curse and gestured toward the cabin. "Get in and stay there." The order was spoken in a low growl of barely controlled anger.

She went in, threw the bolt across the door and ran to the window in time to see Brody disappear completely into the deeper shadows of the forest. She listened but heard nothing other than the soft moan of the wind through the valley.

The stark beauty of the landscape emphasized the loneliness of her life. A sense of isolation swept over her. Being in love, not being loved in return, made it so much more poignant. No one wanted her. It was a simple fact.

Poor little rich girl.

She sucked in a deep breath and concentrated on the view from the window where she stood. From it she could see most of the valley. The sheep had bedded down for the night, fuzzy blurs against the dark shadow of the earth. She realized there was no moon. That's why the sky seemed so black.

Clouds were moving in over the high peaks. She could discern where they stopped by the lack of stars. The rising wind whispered of the storm to come before morning.

The goose bumps rankled along her arms again. She was aware of feeling nervy and tense, ready for danger or disaster.

An hour passed. Another.

Brody didn't return. Her anxiety increased as the storm grew closer. Lightning flashed. Four seconds later, she heard the thunder. The storm was a mile away.

The hot clouds moved closer, obscuring the stars as far as she could see. The lightning burned zigzagged trails over the heavens that seemed to linger after the bolt blinked out. Thunder banged directly overhead and rolled away down the valley.

Then, in a split second of crackling light, she saw what she'd been watching for. Brody, moving across the meadow at great speed, heading for the cabin, the rifle in hand.

She rushed to the door and lifted the bar, then released the bolt. She strained to see what was happening through the narrow slit she allowed as she cautiously opened the door.

The heat lightning blasted over the sky almost continuously now. She saw the running figure again, heading for the cabin. She tensed, wondering if she should let him in. Only if it was Brody. He would have to identify himself—

A shot rang out. Then another.

Her heart skipped, then pounded out of control. A pause in the storm reflected the silence in the meadow. She saw someone walking toward the cabin. This time she knew who the person was. She opened the door and stepped back. Brody came inside.

He threw off his jacket and pulled a walkie-talkie from his belt. He spoke to a guy named Joe. "Did you get him?"

"We did." The other man was laughing. "You wouldn't believe how."

"Tell me," Brody ordered, the frown smoothing out.

"The guy got the drop on Mac. I was hidden in the trees wondering if I could shoot him without getting

Mac killed when this little guy, one of your woollies who thinks he's a goat, came bounding over and butted the dude in the back of the knees. Mac grabbed the gun and wrenched it away. End of fight."

"Good work. Take him to the ranch. We'll meet you there in an hour." Brody clicked off and turned to Jessica. "It's over."

She wrapped her arms around him and clung for dear life. "Who?" she asked.

"We're going to ask the guy my detectives caught." Brody shook his head. "I can't believe he was going to try the same trick he used before. Amateur."

"Right," Jessica agreed, weak with relief that Brody hadn't been hurt. She'd been so afraid for him.

He must have felt her tremor. His voice dropped from elation to assurance. "You're safe, Jess. This will put an end to the danger. You'll be okay now."

She nodded.

"Come on. We're going to the house."

"What about the flock?" She eyed the storm and thought of hail and icy winds.

He chuckled. "Watch it. You're beginning to sound like a rancher's wife."

"I am a rancher's wife."

His glance was skeptical as he handed her jacket to her and grabbed his own. He checked the hot plate. "Ready?"

"My clothes." She went into the bedroom and packed her knapsack with the clothes she'd worn earlier. "Ready," she reported, returning to the living room.

They made it to the ranch house in good time. Two county cruisers were there. Nick Dorelli talked on his radio to someone in dispatch. The sheriff stood on the porch with a cup of coffee in his hand. The prisoner lounged with insolent ease against the porch railing. His hands were cuffed behind him.

Jessica started in surprise.

"Do you know him?" Brody asked.

She swallowed the lump that insisted on forming in her throat. "Clive Grainger. He was my bodyguard before I hired you. He and the woman who went through my clothes worked as partners."

"Nick, Sheriff, did you get that?" He gestured toward Grainger. The men nodded. "Get inside, Jess. The rain is heading this way." Brody told her.

"Brody, Homicide is on the way. He'll be picked up within minutes," Nick reported.

"Good."

Jessica shivered as chills spread throughout her body. The cold gathered around her heart. She went inside and stayed. The police left. She prepared a pot of coffee and poured a cup. She took it to the table and sat down to wait for Brody. There were questions to be asked and answered.

After the deputy's vehicle cleared the bend in the driveway, Brody came in. He studied her while pouring a cup of coffee, then joined her at the table. "My men will stay the night, then head back to Denver tomorrow."

"Why would Grainger want to kill me?" she asked.

"Money."

"Uncle Jesse—"

"Sleeping like a baby. He never heard a thing."

"Isn't the sheriff going to arrest him?"

"The perp hasn't named his accomplice." Brody hesitated. "Let's go to bed. I've had enough running around in the dark and cold to last me a lifetime."

Her lips trembled when she tried to smile at his wry grimace. She should be relieved. They'd caught the man who'd been trying to kill her. All she felt was dread. Soon she would find out who wanted her dead. It would be a hard truth. Brody's eyes were filled with pity. He already knew. So did she.

She changed from her sweat suit to her lavender pajamas while Brody took a warm shower. He held her when he got into bed, but didn't try to make love. It was a long time before either of them went to sleep.

The call came before dawn. Brody took it. "This is her husband. I'll take the message." He listened, then, "Okay, I got it. We'll be there this afternoon if possible."

"What?" she asked when he hung up and looked at her.

"Your grandfather had a massive heart attack during the night. He didn't make it."

Jessica laid her purse on the table in the library and sat at the walnut desk that had belonged to Robert Lacey who had fought beside George Washington in the revolution. Her grandfather had died without a will, and she had been tied up in legal meetings for a month since the funeral.

It was odd—she was the owner of this house and all it contained. She always had been. Her grandmother had stipulated that her husband have the use of it for his lifetime, but it and all her holdings belonged to Jessica.

Her uncle had lingered by her side during the ordeal. Brody hadn't objected. Neither had she.

Since there was no real proof other than a suspicious cut in a tire tread and the fact that he'd been carrying a gun, the man they'd found on the ranch had been charged with trespassing and carrying an unregistered weapon. He'd paid his bail and disappeared. So had the woman who'd been his partner.

Brody entered the room and paced in front of the desk. His dark gaze roamed her face as if looking for cracks or other signs of her falling apart. She returned his stare with stoic calm.

"How are you?" he asked. His tone was kind.

She could take wry or sardonic or harsh from him, but not kind. Kindness was what one showed to strangers in distress.

"Fine. I thought I'd go through the desk and get it cleaned out today. I need to pay the household bills. It's odd. Grandfather wouldn't let the housekeeper or even his accountant do it. He took care of his finances himself."

Brody nodded. "Mind if I sit here and read?" He gestured at the morning newspaper on a nearby table.

"No. Are you keeping an eye on me?"

He flashed her one of his sardonic glances. "That's what I'm paid to do, isn't it?"

"Yes." She toyed with the pen. "I suppose we need to come to a new arrangement...now that I no longer need protection."

Brody settled in a leather chair facing the desk. His poise was one of ease, hands in his pockets, his long legs stretched out and crossed at the ankles. He studied her, his eyes dark and rather moody, giving away nothing.

When they'd arrived last month, he'd gone to his previous quarters instead of following her to her room. She realized it had probably been an awkward situation for him. But maybe not.

Brody lived by his own rules and a false sense of etiquette or social niceties wasn't one of them. She didn't know if he would have stayed with her if she'd requested it.

Perhaps he would have as part of this kinder, gentler Brody she was seeing, the one she didn't like. With the old Brody, she would have known where she stood. But of course, her whole life was different now.

"What makes you think you no longer need protection?" he asked with a return of his cynical edge.

"I know the truth."

That got his attention. He sat up straight and leaned forward, his forearms on his thighs. "What truth?"

"My grandfather was the one who wanted me out of the way." She met his gaze without faltering. She'd steeled herself to deal with this fact soon after they received the call about his heart attack, which had confirmed her suspicions. The man Nick Dorelli had said would be picked up had been her grandfather.

Exposure was something he couldn't have borne. If the shock of knowing he'd been found out hadn't killed him, she thought he would have taken his own life rather than face trial.

She looked away from Brody's penetrating study. Outside, it was a perfect June day. The sun was shining. The breeze was warm and gentle. It was summer in the land, but it was winter in her heart.

He didn't reply, only looked at her with that terrible pity in his gaze.

"You knew almost from the first, didn't you?"

He hesitated before speaking. "I had my suspicions." Again his tone was kind.

"That's why you agreed to the marriage—to get me

out of this house—and why you insisted we live at the ranch.''

"Yes."

A shiver swept over her at his blunt confession. She'd been a blind, trusting fool.

Brody reached for the phone, hit the intercom button and ordered coffee. His eyes never left her. Jessica rubbed her arms and considered the past. Neither of them spoke.

The housekeeper brought the coffee. "I have a fresh apple strudel. Shall I serve that? You didn't eat breakfast,'' she reminded Jessica.

"Yes," Brody agreed before she could refuse.

The housekeeper bustled out, leaving the coffee on the sideboard. Brody poured them each a cup.

When he placed hers on the desk, she tilted her head back and stared at him, hungry for things only he could give her. His glance caught hers before she could look away. His eyes darkened. For the longest minute, he gazed at her while she waited. Longing became an unbearable pressure in her chest.

He straightened and returned to his chair with his cup.

The housekeeper brought the treat and served them. Jessica thanked her. She ate, hardly tasting the perfect pastry or succulent filling. Brody was silent, too.

"I trusted him," she said. "I loved him. I tried so hard to please him when I was sent here to live after my mother's death. I wanted him to be glad to have me—"

Brody visibly tensed. He set the dessert plate aside and again watched her as if he expected her to fall apart.

"You knew. That's why my uncle wasn't arrested at the ranch. You knew he had nothing to do with it."

He nodded, his gaze never faltering.

"Why didn't you tell me?"

"I had hoped you would never find out."

"Why?"

"What good does it do?"

"I should have known," she insisted.

"If I'd tried to tell you, would you have believed me?"

The icy patch on her heart accumulated like winter snow in the Arctic. The chill reached clear to her soul.

Many fine nuances that she'd never recognized came to mind now that she'd faced the truth. "I think my uncle knew I was in danger. Why didn't he do something?"

Brody shrugged. "Your grandfather was cunning. He had the right friends, thanks to your grandmother."

She looked away from Brody's direct gaze. "Did he marry her for her money?"

"From all accounts, he was a social climber and fortune hunter. No matter how much money he might make on his own, he came from the wrong side of the tracks. He would never have been invited into the inner sanctum of society and high finance without your grandmother's name. She was old money."

"Money," Jessica repeated.

"The *love* of money," Brody reminded her.

"I thought he cared for me. He was reserved and rather rigid, but I thought he cared."

"Parents are supposed to love their children and put them first. Your grandfather wasn't blood kin," he reminded her, as if this might make it easier to accept the fact that the person she'd depended on for nurturing since she was twelve had tried to have her killed.

Brody's mother sent him off alone to live with a distant relative he didn't know when he was fourteen. He knew what she was feeling, how deep the sense of betrayal went. He'd been through it when he'd been little more than a boy. At least she had a degree of maturity on her side to soften the blow.

Anger, irrational and destructive, made her want to lash out at the mother who had hurt him. The love of a child was a gift, a most precious thing. To throw it away...

A heart was a terrible thing to waste.

"I've talked to a local judge, an old friend of the family, actually. He says I won't have any trouble in setting aside the will." She drew a careful breath so that she could say the next part. "We can arrange for a divorce at any time."

Brody didn't move for a long second, then he nodded.

"I'll pay you for the year—"

"Forget that." His face darkened.

"You may as well take it gracefully. I'll simply have the money transferred to your account and keep doing it until you give up. You saved my life, Brody. It isn't something I shall ever forget."

He muttered an expletive, shocking her.

# Chapter Fourteen

Brody set the cup aside. The rage he'd rarely felt except in relation to Jessica rose in him. He would have choked her grandfather with his bare hands if the coward hadn't died first.

For Jessica's sake, he was glad things had worked out this way. It had saved her from going through a lengthy, tabloid-hyped trial. There would have been a TV miniseries, no doubt.

He tried to assess her emotional state, but she disclosed nothing. It was something he'd witnessed in her before—this ability to shut herself completely off, to smile and talk and act as if she hadn't a care in the world, even when she knew someone was trying to kill her. She'd never said a word to her society friends, had never asked for help or pity from anyone.

She never would.

A sudden need to touch her had him gritting his

teeth. He wouldn't impose himself on her, but he wished she would turn to him... Forget it. She no longer needed him. That much was clear. She hadn't come to him once since that silent flight and their return to this house. He was a hired gun and now his duty was finished.

The anger swept over him again. That was the last thing she needed from him. He headed for the door. "I'm going for a walk."

She nodded in her well-brought-up manner.

Jessica was a lady, he mused, standing on the patio. She'd never cause a scene or engage in a shouting match. Only in his arms did she go wild, shrieking and moaning her ecstasy when they made love.

Now he sensed she was buried inside herself, withdrawing more each moment as she became the lady of the manor again, rather than a rancher's wife.

A hard fist of need slammed into his chest. He'd miss that woman. He hadn't let himself depend on anyone in years. He'd learned that lesson the hard way. But...he'd miss her.

After a long walk he returned to the house, made a couple of calls, showered and packed. "I'm off," he said, stopping at the door of the library where Jessica bent over her books and wrote out the household checks.

She looked up, that one slender eyebrow, the one with the attitude, rising as she silently questioned him.

"I have a reservation on the three-o'clock flight. I'm wasting my time here." He smiled. "I do have a business to run and a ranch to rusticate on, so I'm heading out."

"I see."

No fake protests, no forced explanations. Just that cool acceptance. A class act all the way.

"Keep me posted."

"I will. Brody...?"

"Yeah?"

She licked her lips. "Thank you. For everything."

"Nada. It was nothing."

He watched her, not sure what he was looking for. Mentally shaking his head at his own vulnerability where she was concerned—yeah, he admitted it; she got to him in a way no other person ever had since he'd been grown—he gave her a half salute and headed out. The family driver was there with the car. He jumped in and told him to head for the airport.

"We're going down for the rodeo. You want to come?"

Brody looked up from the report he was reading. The cowboy leaned in the door to the ranch house and looked at him with all the eagerness of youth in his smile. The young pup.

"No, thanks, I have plans. You boys have a good time. I'll come bail you out on Monday if you're not back at the ranch."

The grin in the tanned, lightly freckled face broadened. "We'll be back on time. We got our girls with us."

Brody sketched a farewell and watched the students prepare to leave. It was a new world. He'd allowed his summer hands to invite their girls up for the Fourth of July celebration. The girls were visiting for the entire week. And staying in the bunkhouse with the guys. Aunt Essie wouldn't have approved, although she would have liked the idea of hiring females as wranglers.

The couples' laughter as they piled into the old pickup floated in the open windows, making him realize his years. Thirty-three and he felt old clear to the bone.

Forcing his attention to the wrap-up of an important case, he finished the report, tossed it on the coffee table and strode out on the back porch. Don closed the paddock gate and ambled over to the porch.

"Warm today," he commented. He wiped the sweat from his face with his sleeve.

"Yeah."

"You not going to town?"

"Nah."

"Hmm."

Brody grimaced at the disapproval in the older man's tone. He thought Brody should have brought Jessica home and had shown his disgust by rarely speaking for the past week.

"I could hardly kidnap her." Brody voiced his thoughts.

"You could have asked her if she wanted to come. You got any tea? I'm out."

Brody poured two glasses and took them outside. They sat on the porch, legs dangling and leaned against the support posts.

"Why don't you call and find out what she's doing over the holiday? She might like to come out for the rodeo."

"Why don't you? You're the one with the hots for her," he snarled, his temper exploding as frustration and hunger beat at him with the fury of an angry mob.

"I would, but I'm not her husband. She picked you, Lord knows why."

Brody snorted. He knew why. She'd needed his protection. She'd paid well for his services. He had the savings account to prove it. He'd done his job. When no longer needed, he'd left.

Simple.

He just wished he didn't feel like hell all the time. Or that he could sleep one night through. He sighed.

"Call her."

"No."

"Stubborn." Don set the empty glass on the porch none too gently and returned to the llamas, which he was checking for pink eye. Brody noticed a green stain on the back of his shirt.

He took the glasses in and put them in the dishwasher, then paced the kitchen restlessly. Oh, hell, it wouldn't hurt to call. She was probably at a lawn party or something like that anyway. He wouldn't get to talk to her.

The telephone rang several times before the housekeeper answered.

"Uh, this is Brody Smith. Is Jessica in?"

"She's at the hospital."

"Hospital," he croaked.

"Visiting," the housekeeper quickly added. "She visits the sick children. She always takes them gifts on holidays, you know."

No, he didn't know. There were lots of things still to be discovered about his wife, not that he'd get a chance to discover them, but— "I'm sorry. What was that?"

"I asked when you were coming back. Jessica is very lonely. I think she misses you."

"Not me," he started to say. His heart began to beat very hard. "Is she...do you think she's unhappy?"

"Well, sometimes she stays out at night. Henry said she used to stand for hours at the windows in the Lockhart Building. She has been driving herself of late, so we don't know where she goes. Her eyes are sad."

"I see. Well, tell her I called. The rodeo is going on over the holiday weekend. I thought she might like to attend."

"I'll tell her."

After they hung up, he stood there, worry eating at him. It was none of his business. That day in the library she'd made it clear she no longer needed him. He'd been expecting to hear something on the divorce any day.

He paced a while longer, then picked up the phone. Nothing like making a total fool of yourself, but he had to check for himself, just to be sure.

Jessica stepped out of the elevator. The building was silent, empty the way she liked it. It was almost two o'clock in the morning. Her favorite hour of the day. Or night.

The loneliest hour.

She pressed a hand to her aching breast. A person got over things. She knew that. Time was the key. She would simply outwait the longing and the loneliness. In a year or so, she was thinking of adopting a child. When she could be sure that her reasons were the right ones.

Leaning against the railing, she rested her forehead on the cool glass and watched the traffic far below. A cab stopped and let a passenger out. Another person grabbed the cab before a couple jumped in. The man shook his fist at the departing vehicle. She smiled wryly. Life in the city…

Her sigh steamed the glass, but the moisture was quickly gone as the cool breeze from the air conditioning wafted over her. The trees in the atrium swayed and rustled.

Inside she was aware of the cold, a tiny frozen spot that would never thaw.

Poor little rich girl.

She tried to laugh, but the sound was hoarse. She pressed her palms against the glass and felt the cold spread over her hands.

The reflection in the glass changed. She stared, puzzled, then she realized the elevator doors had opened. A man stepped out. She turned slowly and watched him approach.

"Are you real?" she asked.

Brody stopped in front of her. "Touch me and see," he invited in a sexy tone that caused shivers to dart through her.

He didn't smile. In fact, he looked so solemn she worried about the news he'd come all this way to tell her. Brody didn't travel a thousand miles to discuss the weather.

She laid her hands on his chest. He covered them with his.

"Cold hands, warm heart," he murmured. The smile appeared, brushing his lips lightly, and was gone.

"What are you doing here?"

His chest lifted in a deep breath. "I've come to take you home. To the ranch. If you want to come."

She blinked, uncertain of his meaning. "Why?"

"There's a rodeo in town. I thought you might like to see it." He frowned as if the answer displeased him.

Her heart butted her rib cage like Ram in one of his boisterous moods. "Why?" she insisted.

"I've missed you."

"I see." He missed her? Or the sex? Or the cooking? "You'll come?"

She shook her head. He looked away, but not before she'd seen something dark and hurting in his eyes. She pressed her hands against his chest as need, urgent and hopeful, filled her. "Why, Brody?"

He swallowed. He dropped his hands to his sides, his fists clenched so tight his knuckles turned white. "I've missed you," he said again, but with an edge of desperation.

She suppressed the wild joy in her heart. She had to know more, to be sure she understood exactly what he was saying. "In bed? In the kitchen?" She managed a light laugh, the one she'd learned early so that no one would know how she felt.

Brody caught her shoulders, his movement so fast she was startled out of her society smile.

"In my life," he said in a low, hoarse tone that seemed ripped from his guts. "In my arms." He clenched his teeth for a second, then said, "In my heart."

She stared at him, speechless. For all her wishing, she hadn't really let herself think he might love her. But now she couldn't deny the possibility. This moment was crucial. She had to say the right thing, or else he'd leave and never return. She didn't even know how she knew this, but she did.

She closed her eyes, afraid to show the need. "Take me home, Brody. Please."

She was engulfed in a hug that threatened to crack every rib she possessed. She didn't feel a thing. There were other sensations to marvel over—the feel of his mouth on hers, his caresses all over her back, his hand fisted in her hair, his chest warm and solid against her breasts—so many things.

"Let's go," he said.

"Now?"

"You got something else to do?" he demanded.

She loved the brashness, the masculine arrogance behind the question, the startling quality of his smile, the light in his eyes...oh, yes, the light in his eyes most especially.

"Brody, I love you." She gazed up at him anxiously, afraid she'd scare him away with her confession.

He returned her gaze for a long moment. "If it's a tenth of what I feel, it'll be enough to last a lifetime."

"Does that mean what I think it means?"

"I love you, Jessica Lacey Lockhart Smith." His eyes darkened. "Be sure you want this. I'll never let you go once I take you home."

Her smile was radiant. "I'll never want to leave."

Jessica sat on her favorite rock and watched the activity below. The llamas were being loaded onto a truck to be returned to their native country. One of the Andean tribes was taking them as part of a breeding program for their developing wool market.

Voices rose from the valley and came to her on the October breeze. The cottonwoods along the creeks and the aspens girdling the hills were buttery yellow now that their leaves had turned. She heard Brody cursing as the stubborn llama male decided he didn't want to relocate.

She laughed. When they got the animals loaded,

Brody washed his hands at the horse trough and scrubbed the green stain on his shirt with his handkerchief. Then he hiked up the inclined rimrock to her.

She made room for him to sit behind her to watch the sunset. He swung a jeans-clad leg over the boulder and took his place. She leaned against him contentedly. But not for long. As usual when they touched, the need became too much.

"Ready?" he asked.

"Yes."

They ambled down the path to the ranch house. The scent of simmering chicken and dumplings and freshly baked cinnamon rolls welcomed them into the house. "Supper first?" she asked.

"Yes."

She studied him while she set the places. He had a mysterious gleam in his eyes.

"I'll miss the llamas," she said.

"The stud had to go. He took to spitting on me every chance he got. There's room for only two males who are in love with you on this ranch. A third was too much."

She lifted one eyebrow in question.

He grinned. "Me and Ram. Well, Don, too, but he's better at hiding it."

Happiness bubbled in her. She couldn't ever remember being so happy. There was one other thing she wanted. She'd tell her handsome husband later. In bed.

They watched the news and commented on the weather, always an important item for a rancher. The anticipation built. Brody was deliberately dragging out the evening. She could wait.

At ten-thirty, he stood and stretched. After clicking

off the TV, he gestured that she should go first. She floated up the stairs.

He read a couple of faxes in his office while she prepared for bed. When she climbed between the sheets, he came over and kissed her, then turned out the lights. He pulled down the room-darkening shades before heading for the bathroom.

A bit puzzled, she watched him until he disappeared inside. The shower came on. A few minutes later, she heard the hum of his electric razor. Then silence.

The bathroom door opened. The room was so dark she couldn't see a thing. "Brody?" she questioned, worry creeping in.

A strange light appeared. She raised up on her elbows and watched it float toward her. Then she heard Brody's voice as he hummed a melody she'd never heard. The eerie glow bobbed and swayed in time to the tune as if engaged in a secret ritual.

She realized what was happening.

Clamping a hand over her mouth didn't help. She giggled and chortled helplessly as the show continued. The tune ended and the glow dipped down, then up. She applauded as her sexy husband took a bow.

She heard him take two steps. There were two corresponding bobs of the glow, then the covers lifted and Brody's masculine length covered her.

"Thank you," she murmured as he planted kisses on her face. "It was a delightful show."

"It isn't over." He kissed her senseless, until she writhed in hunger under him and begged him to come to her. Finally he pushed up on his arms. "Observe, madam."

She watched the glow disappear as his body merged

with hers. It reminded her of her earlier idea. "When are we going to start a child?" she asked.

He settled himself deep in her. "When do you want to?"

"Soon." She moved against him.

"Tonight is fine with me." His voice was husky, with a quiet undertone that spoke of love and his faith in her not to abuse that love. The gift of a heart...

Tears filled her eyes, and she was glad of the dark so he wouldn't see. "Yes."

He shifted to her side. The condom shrank to a limp glow and was tossed aside. Then he came into her again, flesh against flesh, heart to heart, soul joined to soul. He made the sweetest, gentlest love to her, then held her while their breathing quieted.

She thought of a child growing inside her. Brody must have, too. He rubbed her stomach as if it already was rounded with the new life. There would be many children on the ranch next year. Besides their own, they were going to open the ranch to other children. The Lockhart-Smith Foundation would oversee the program for kids to get a new chance on life.

Jessica sighed, unable to believe her happiness.

"Yeah," her husband murmured, his breath warm on her temple. "Life is good."

And so it was.

\* \* \* \* \*

# *Daniel MacGregor is at it again...*

## *New York Times* bestselling author

# NORA ROBERTS

introduces us to a new generation of MacGregors
as the lovable patriarch of the illustrious MacGregor
clan plays matchmaker again, this time to his three
gorgeous granddaughters in

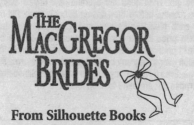

# THE MACGREGOR BRIDES

**From Silhouette Books**

Don't miss this brand-new continuation of Nora Roberts's
enormously popular *MacGregor* miniseries.

Available November 1997 at your favorite retail outlet.

# Take 4 bestselling love stories FREE

## Plus get a FREE surprise gift!

## Special Limited-time Offer

**Mail to Silhouette Reader Service™**

3010 Walden Avenue
P.O. Box 1867
Buffalo, N.Y. 14240-1867

**YES!** Please send me 4 free Silhouette Special Edition® novels and my free surprise gift. Then send me 6 brand-new novels every month, which I will receive months before they appear in bookstores. Bill me at the low price of $3.34 each plus 25¢ delivery and applicable sales tax, if any.* That's the complete price and a savings of over 10% off the cover prices—quite a bargain! I understand that accepting the books and gift places me under no obligation ever to buy any books. I can always return a shipment and cancel at any time. Even if I never buy another book from Silhouette, the 4 free books and the surprise gift are mine to keep forever.

235 BPA A3UV

| Name | (PLEASE PRINT) | |
|------|----------------|---|
| Address | Apt. No. | |
| City | State | Zip |

This offer is limited to one order per household and not valid to present Silhouette Special Edition® subscribers. *Terms and prices are subject to change without notice. Sales tax applicable in N.Y.

USPED-696                    ©1990 Harlequin Enterprises Limited

# As seen on TV!
# *Free Gift Offer*

With a Free Gift proof-of-purchase from any Silhouette® book,
you can receive a beautiful cubic zirconia pendant.

This gorgeous marquise-shaped stone is a genuine cubic
zirconia—accented by an 18" gold tone necklace.

(Approximate retail value $19.95)

# Send for yours today...

## compliments of ▼ *Silhouette*®
TM

To receive your free gift, a cubic zirconia pendant, send us one original proof-of-
purchase, photocopies not accepted, from the back of any Silhouette Romance™,
Silhouette Desire®, Silhouette Special Edition®, Silhouette Intimate Moments®
or Silhouette Yours Truly™ title available at your favorite retail outlet, together with
the Free Gift Certificate, plus a check or money order for $1.65 U.S./$2.15 CAN. (do
not send cash) to cover postage and handling, payable to Silhouette Free Gift Offer.
We will send you the specified gift. Allow 6 to 8 weeks for delivery. Offer good until
December 31, 1997, or while quantities last. Offer valid in the U.S. and Canada only.

## *Free Gift Certificate*

Name: _____

Address: _____

City: _____ State/Province: _____ Zip/Postal Code: _____

Mail this certificate, one proof-of-purchase and a check or money order for postage
and handling to: SILHOUETTE FREE GIFT OFFER 1997. In the U.S.: 3010 Walden
Avenue, P.O. Box 9077, Buffalo NY 14269-9077. In Canada: P.O. Box 613, Fort Erie,
Ontario L2Z 5X3.

---

## FREE GIFT OFFER                         084-KFD
ONE PROOF-OF-PURCHASE
To collect your fabulous FREE GIFT, a cubic zirconia pendant, you must include this
original proof-of-purchase for each gift with the properly completed Free Gift Certificate.

---

084-KFDR

## ELIZABETH AUGUST

Continues the twelve-book
series—36 HOURS—in
November 1997 with
Book Five

# CINDERELLA STORY

Life was hardly a fairy tale for Nina Lindstrom. Out of work
and with an ailing child, the struggling single mom was
running low on hope. Then Alex Bennett solved her problems
with one convenient proposal: marriage. And though he had
made no promises beyond financial security, Nina couldn't
help but feel that with a little love, happily-ever-afters really
could come true!

For Alex and Nina and *all* the residents of Grand Springs,
Colorado, the storm-induced blackout was just the beginning
of 36 Hours that changed *everything!* You won't want to miss a
single book.

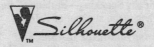

Share in the joy of yuletide romance with brand-new
stories by two of the genre's most beloved writers

DIANA PALMER

and

JOAN JOHNSTON

in

# LONE STAR CHRISTMAS

Diana Palmer and Joan Johnston share their favorite
Christmas anecdotes and personal stories in this
*special hardbound edition.*

Diana Palmer delivers an irresistible spin-off of her
**LONG, TALL TEXANS** series and Joan Johnston crafts an
unforgettable new chapter to **HAWK'S WAY** in this wonderful
keepsake edition celebrating the holiday season. So
perfect for gift giving, you'll want one for yourself...and
one to give to a special friend!

Available in November at your favorite retail outlet!

Only from

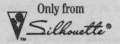

Silhouette®